DUCK SEASON DEATH

DUCK SEASON DEATH

June Wright

INTRODUCTION BY DERHAM GROVES

**DARK
PASSAGE**

VERSE CHORUS PRESS

A Dark Passage book
Published by Verse Chorus Press
PO Box 14806, Portland OR 97293
info@versechorus.com

Cover design by Mike Reddy
Interior design and layout by Steve Connell/Transgraphic
Artwork on facing page by Emilie Jane Wright
Dark Passage logo by Mike Reddy

Printed in the USA

Library of Congress Cataloging-in-Publication Data

Wright, June, 1919-2012.
  Duck season death / June Wright ; introduction by Derham Groves.
    pages ; cm
    ISBN 978-1-891241-35-2 (softcover) — ISBN 978-1-891241-98-7 (ebook)
I. Groves, Derham. II.Title.
  PR9619.3.W727D83 2014
  823'.914—dc23
                                    2014044112

JUNE
WRIGHT

DUCK SEASON DEATH

INTRODUCTION

The crime novels of Australian author June Wright (1919–2012) have been unfairly forgotten, and in my view thoroughly merit a fresh reassessment. The mother of six children had six books published by Hutchinson in London between 1948 and 1966. "June demonstrates herself to be both mentally and physically fertile," observed the outspoken journalist Beth Thwaites in *The Truth* newspaper in Melbourne, Victoria. Interesting locations, spirited female characters and believable social settings are characteristic of all of June's murder mysteries.

After June's first child, Patrick, was born in 1942, "to combat the lack of mental exercise, I haunted the local lending library for reading matter," June recalled in 1997. "But, owing to the war, there was not a large supply . . . I read all of the novels by Frances Parkinson Keyes and a new authoress called Monica Dickens. Dynastic epics covering generations of English family life soon dried up. Agatha Christie was a favourite; Mignon Eberhart, a skilled performer of the 'Had I but known' school, more so. That's it, I thought after a period of re-reads. I'll write my own!"

Being an avid reader of crime fiction, June knew precisely how to proceed. "You must drop your clues, like stitches, on the way out, and pick them up neatly in a pattern when you're coming in," she told the Australian magazine *Woman's Day* in 1948. "The clues give the reader a chance and you mustn't fool him with any misleading trickery. You must have a plausible plot and the murderer must get an honourable mention early in the book, although you never let the reader into his mental processes. There must be no coincidences or unaccountable solutions."

June had to juggle writing with looking after her husband, Stewart, and their six children: Patrick, Rosemary, Nicholas, Anthony, Brenda and Stephen. Six nights a week (her one night "off" was spent ironing clothes!), after the children had gone to bed, she escaped to her study to write for two or three hours, come what may, when "the dozens of ideas she has while peeling potatoes and washing nappies spill from her brain into print," wrote Lisa Allan of *The Argus* newspaper in Melbourne. "And therein are the two essential ingredients for writing [June] says—patience and perseverance. 'It's easy to dash off 200 inspired words, but the other 80,000 to finish the book aren't always so quick in coming.'" Writing about 1,000 words in longhand per night, the first draft of a book usually took June three or four months to complete, "unless something cataclysmic happens to the family in the meantime," she told the author of "Housewife's Recipe for Murder" (1958).

June's first crime novel, *Murder in the Telephone Exchange* (1948), was set in the Central Telephone Exchange in Melbourne, where she had worked as a telephonist during World War II. In this book Sarah Compton, a supervisor, is bashed to death with a "buttinsky," a gadget used by telephone mechanics to interrupt telephone conversations. Maggie Byrnes, a gutsy young telephonist at the exchange (like June was), narrates the fast-moving whodunit, which outsold Agatha Christie's novels in Australia in 1948. (Verse Chorus Press reissued *Murder in the Telephone Exchange* in 2014.)

Most book reviewers were full of praise for June's maiden effort. However, she was completely floored by the following slap on the knuckles from A.R. McElwain, the influential crime fiction reviewer for two widely read daily newspapers, *The Advertiser* in Adelaide, South Australia, and *The Herald* in Melbourne, whom June later described as "a devotee of the detective story and a zealous guardian of its mores." "Above all, Miss [sic] Wright must never again aggravate the honest student's blood-pressure by resorting to a low,

JUNE WRIGHT IN 1952

inexcusable trick to lead him off on the wrong track—right there on page one at that," wrote McElwain in his review of *Murder in the Telephone Exchange*. This led to a friendly exchange of letters between the author and the reviewer. McElwain encouraged June to read *The Art of the Mystery Story* (1946) edited by Howard Haycraft. "It is the best anthology of practically everything good that has been written about detection stories and contains criticism and hints by all of the dons of the craft," he said. June henceforth regarded McElwain as her literary guide.

So Bad a Death (1949), June's second murder mystery, also features Maggie Byrnes, who is now married to John Matheson, a police inspector whom she met during the investigation of Sarah Compton's murder. In this book the newlyweds rent "Dower House" in Middleburn, a fictitious Melbourne suburb, which was based on Ashburton, the real Melbourne suburb where June lived at the time. Despite Middleburn's outward gentility, it proves to be a hotbed of crime. *So Bad a Death* was serialised on ABC radio and also in *Woman's Day*.

June's third book, *The Devil's Caress* (1952), is more of a psychological thriller than a whodunit. It features Marsh Mowbray, an attractive young GP, who is unwittingly pitted against her boss, Katherine Waring, a Senior Honorary Physician at the hospital where she works, and Katherine's husband Kingsley, a leading Melbourne surgeon, while staying at the Warings' beach house at Matthews, a fictitious hamlet on the Mornington Peninsula in Victoria. "Mrs. Wright's reportage is as ever brisk and competent," commended A.R. McElwain in his review of *The Devil's Caress*. "But I eagerly await the day when she concentrates more upon genuine, plausible detection and less upon melodramatic situations."

For her fourth crime novel, *Reservation for Murder* (1958), June created the unassuming but strong-willed Catholic nun-detective Mother Mary St. Paul of the Cross – Mother Paul for short. She was based on Mother Mary Dorothea Devine (1900–1990), a Sister of Charity who was the head of the maternity ward at St. Vincent's

Hospital in Melbourne when June gave birth to twins there in 1946. In *Reservation for Murder* Mother Paul is in charge of Kilcomoden, a hostel for office girls and secretaries near Melbourne, which is also the scene of a murder and an apparent suicide. John Long, an imprint of Hutchinson, published this book. Writing didn't make June rich; the royalties from *Reservation for Murder* paid for new sliding doors in the Wrights' living room.

June's fifth and sixth crime novels, *Faculty of Murder* (1961) and *Make-Up for Murder* (1966), also feature the inimitable Mother Paul. In *Faculty of Murder* the nun-detective runs Brigit Moore Hall, a fictitious Catholic women's college at the University of Melbourne (the tower of Ormond College was on the book's dust jacket). Mother Paul investigates the disappearance of a college resident and the death of a professor's wife. In *Make-Up for Murder* the nun-detective is in charge of Maryhill Girls' School in Melbourne. Mother Paul investigates the murder of a former school student and the disappearance of a famous TV singer. June stopped writing crime fiction altogether after that.

While having six crime novels published was a great achievement, June hit a couple of literary brick walls along the way. In 1952 Hutchinson rejected her crime novel *The Law Courts Mystery*, which was set in and around Melbourne's law courts, because "the readers reported that although your book was likeable, with humour and movement, it was spoilt by the plot, which was unconvincing and rather muddled. Also, the relationship between the characters, even when they have a lot to do with each other, is always too remote and bloodless," June's publisher told her. *The Law Courts Mystery* was never published and the manuscript has now been lost.

On the basis of three critical readers' reports Hutchinson also rejected the crime novel that June wrote following *Reservation for Murder,* which was called *Duck Season Death.* The first reader said: "There are very good features here, but the author . . . has in effect produced a rather stock-box novel of the whodunit house

THE TEXTBOOK DETECTIVE STORY

DUCK SEASON DEATH

BY

Dorothy Daniel

June Wright

written about 1955

& rejected by Hutchinson's — submitted elsewhere — hence pseudonym — and also rejected.

party variety." In the second reader's opinion, "if the author had strewn less red herrings around, her mystery would have been less confused and in consequence improved." And the third reader said: "The mechanics of this story follow the old lines of the 'country house' murder, where everyone is suspect and the final denouement highlights the most insignificant character." However, June's book is much better and far more interesting than the readers' criticisms suggest.

In *Duck Season Death* Athol Sefton, the publisher of an Australian literary magazine called *Culture and Critic,* is fatally shot while duck hunting in northern Victoria with his nephew Charles Carmichael, the crime fiction reviewer for *Culture and Critic,* who then sets out to solve his uncle's murder by using his knowledge of detective stories. June suggested *The Textbook Detective Story* as an alternative title for *Duck Season Death,* and I suspect that her literary guide, the crime fiction reviewer A.R. McElwain, was the inspiration for the character of Carmichael. Furthermore, given Carmichael's particular occupation, I'm sure that the irony of getting three negative, book-deal-shattering reviews of *Duck Season Death* was not lost on June—as disappointed as she must have been to receive them.

The good news is that everyone can now read *Duck Season Death*—albeit more than fifty years after June wrote it. What a marvellous time capsule this book is of everyday life in Australia in the late 1950s, as well as challenging the detective powers of the reader. Let's hope that in the best traditions of Sherlock Holmes pastiches June's family will one day discover *The Law Courts Mystery* hidden in a trunk somewhere in an attic.

DERHAM GROVES

CONTENTS

PART ONE

Shooters and Suspects

I

The summer had been an abnormally wet one. From the Fisheries and Game Department of the State Government of Victoria came a bulletin to the effect that duck-shooters might look forward to an excellent season's sport. Dry conditions in the north had sent flocks of chestnut and grey teal, freckled, wood, hardhead and black duck winging their way south to the lush swamps and reedy lakes scattered below the Murray river.

One of the districts suggested by Game Research officers for the three months of duck-shooting was a radius of fifteen miles centred approximately by the small town of Dunbavin.

About three miles to the northeast of Dunbavin, the country rose out of its swampy bed in a knoll known as Campbell's Hill. Nearly a hundred years previously, a squatter from the wild cattle district further inland had built on the rise a pseudo–hunting box. He used to retire there to escape the importunities of Her Majesty's Colonial Surveyors, and to ease his nostalgia for the grouse moors of his homeland by shooting the plentiful wildfowl. Constructed of sturdy stone, the house had outlasted each subsequent owner who had put it to as many varied and unprofitable uses as there were shoddy additions to its original walls. The present owner, Ellis Bryce, had made it into a hotel catering for duck-shooters.

Ellis was a man of unending wild-cat schemes which he took for inspirations of genius. Indolent by nature, his enthusiasm seldom went beyond the initial idea. Having bought out the previous owner of Campbell's Hill, who had been trying to make a go of rice growing, he satiated his genius by talking the local licensing court into a permit to sell liquor and putting up a hanging sign whose gothic lettering read *The Duck and Dog Inn*. Then he sat back grandly and allowed his sister, Grace, to do all the mundane toil connected with the running of a country pub.

Miss Bryce was devoted to her widowed younger brother, and had followed him into all his projects, lending the resources of both her energy and her meagre income. She was a faded but wiry little woman, pared down to skin and bone by years of unnecessary bustling and fretting.

One humid, rainy day towards the end of February, Miss Bryce sat at Ellis's littered desk in the gunroom checking through the reservations for the opening of the season. Her brother lounged in an armchair in the hall outside, occasionally calling out items which caught his fancy in the local newspaper. He enjoyed pointing up the bucolic journalese by reading in a declamatory manner.

"'A delightful afternoon was had by all at the lovely home of Dr and Mrs Spenser, who opened their beautiful grounds for a Garden Fete in aid of our newly formed and enthusiastic Arts and Crafts Group. Wearing a charming gown of burnt sienna marocain figured with lime green leaves, Mrs Spenser—'"

"Ellis, will you be quiet! How do you expect me to work out the allocation of rooms when you're—We'll have the guests arriving and no notion how to place them and all you can do—You don't seem to realise the amount of work—" Miss Bryce always talked in unfinished sentences, her darting mind in advance of her tongue.

"They'll shuffle down all right," he returned easily. "What is a cloche curvette? Mrs Spenser was wearing a smart brown one."

"Probably her old basin felt, done up," Miss Bryce replied absently. "Ellis, who is this man, Harris P. Jeffrey?"

"'Dr Spenser dispensed hospitality with his customary genial bonhomie.' If his hospitality was anything like the whisky he gave me once, I'd say he dispensed right out of the bottles from his surgery . . . An American, by the sound of his name and the look of the initial. They always seem to have their Christian and surnames the wrong way round."

"An American!" repeated Miss Bryce uncertainly. "Oh dear, and we've only got the one bathroom."

"So what!" Ellis tried out the phrase distastefully, as though ready to make every concession to the visitor's well-being.

"Aren't they rather funny about wanting private bathrooms? I don't know how many times I've told you to install another one, or at least a shower recess. That alcove at the end of the upper passage, and there's the water tank right outside—Ellis, you must bestir yourself. Now see what has happened—an American coming!"

Her reproaches blunted themselves on *The Dunbavin Post.* "'A distressing disturbance to the peace occurred outside Duff's Hotel following the cricket match between Dunbavin Eleven and the visiting team from Jumping Creek on Saturday evening last. Sergeant Motherwell—'"

"I'll put Mr Jeffrey in the room next to the bathroom," decided Miss Bryce, as a solution to the problem. "I see we have the Dougalls coming again. Do you think they would mind if I put them in a smaller room this year? The Happy Holiday Agency made a booking for a two-bedroom and it pays to keep their clients satisfied. A deposit paid too—father and son. Miss Dougall could have her usual room of course. What do you think, Ellis?"

"'In my twenty years as duty officer in this town, declared Sergeant Motherwell, commenting on the situation which could have got out of hand but for his timely appearance on the scene of the commotion—'"

"Ellis!" cried Miss Bryce.

"'—never heard such violent uncontrolled language.' Poor old Motherwell! What does it matter where you put Pukka and Memsahib? They always complain about something, anyway. Which reminds me—there was a telegram from our old friend, Sefton. You'll find it on the desk somewhere. He's bringing his nephew along with him this year."

"Why didn't you tell me before? Now you've upset—you really are the most inconsiderate—" With a long suffering sigh which had no effect whatsoever, Miss Bryce fumbled amongst the bills, receipts and circulars and found the telegram. 'Reserve accommodation for self and nephew, Charles Carmichael, from evening 28th February—Athol Sefton.' As Ellis was now talking to the Duck and Dog's solitary guest, she did not call out for his advice, but marked in two adjoining rooms on the floor plan she had drawn up. She would tell Ellis later what she thought of Mr Sefton's impending sojourn.

The guest—a pale, unobtrusive man called Wilson—had arrived a week earlier. He was evidently not a duck-shooter for he had brought no guns with him; neither had he made any enquiries about local equipment, while he was patently nervous of the two or three water dogs Ellis kept for the use of the guests. Although afflicted with a stammer which made conversation not only embarrassing but tedious, he was no trouble and went off for long walks wearing khaki shorts, which revealed his pale bony legs and a pair of field glasses slung around his plucked chicken neck. Miss Bryce presumed that he was some sort of ornithologist, who did not like to vouchsafe the information because of the terrific effort needed to form the word.

Miss Bryce's distraction became further diverted as her roving eye lighted on an open letter lying on the desk. It was written in bold capitals with a few dashes and twirls to make up the rest of the words. The worry lines on her face waxed as she deciphered it. Presently she turned her head sideways to call out to Ellis about it and almost rubbed noses with Wilson, who had come into the gunroom unheard.

Miss Bryce dismissed the extraordinary notion that he had been looking over her shoulder. "Why, good morning, Mr Wilson! Going out walking again? And it's such a wet day! Good weather for ducks, as so we hope. But you have a raincoat, haven't you?" Unlike her brother, who maliciously delighted in engaging him in conversation, she always kept to questions which required only a nod or shake of Wilson's head. When he had gone, she turned back to the letter. "Ellis, I don't like the sound of this young woman Jerry wants to bring home for the weekend. Who is she?"

"A m-m-model."

"Shh, he'll hear you. And you shouldn't tease him like that. It's most unkind. How would you like—it's a pity you don't pay more attention to your children instead of—it was an artist last time—at least she called herself an artist. I'm sure I couldn't make head nor tail of that painting she gave you. It looked to me as though one of the dogs had got to it. Still, I'm not sure I wouldn't prefer an artist to a model. Why does Jerry get entangled with such females?"

Ellis gave a sudden guffaw. "Not that sort of model. This one's paid to wear clothes."

"I think it is high time you behaved as a father should and not let your children run wild."

"Wild? Shelagh? Now, come, come!"

"Yes, Shelagh is all right, though I must say it doesn't seem right for a girl of twenty-two to be so certain of herself and so—well, sort of unfeeling, even if she is a nurse."

"Yes, I know," said Ellis, yawning. "At least Jerry's females are amusing."

"Ellis, you are the most unnatural father. You've allowed those two to grow up anyhow. It is easy to see whom Jerry takes after. But Shelagh is a good girl. At least she is conscious of her duties and comes home to help at this busy time. That finishes the rooms, thank goodness." Miss Bryce marked a room for Margot Stainsbury as far from Jerry's as possible. "Now for the seating arrangements."

"All this organisation has worn me out," said Ellis. "I think I'll go and open the bar."

"Oh no, you don't. You must decide what we are going to do about Mr Sefton and Major Dougall."

"What about them?"

"We can't have a repetition of last year. In fact, if I had my way we would send a polite letter to Mr Sefton telling him we are booked out this year. He is the most unpleasant man I have ever met—a real trouble-maker for all his grand manner. He was downright insulting to poor Major Dougall. And Mrs Dougall was telling me how he'd deliberately misled them over some investments."

"Put Athol next to Jerry's model," suggested Ellis. "That will keep him occupied."

"And have Jerry making scenes like he did over that artist creature?" she asked scornfully. "Not that it wasn't a very good thing for him that she did get off with Mr Sefton, but—oh dear, how difficult it all is! And you're no help, Ellis. You're as malicious as Mr Sefton. I declare you enjoy seeing everything uncomfortable."

"I admit I find Athol at work not unamusing."

"No doubt you'll still find him amusing when the other guests refuse to stay with him in the house."

"They won't," he said lazily. "The drinks are too good and so is the shooting—and so is your cooking, Grace."

She tried not to look mollified and retorted tartly, "Well, don't blame me if your amusing Mr Sefton one day causes trouble that even you won't find entertaining, Ellis."

II

A cocktail party, Charles Carmichael reflected, is one of the drearier rituals of modern social and commercial life. It was no wonder that critics became either inflated with carbohydrates and self-importance or soul-cynical and dyspeptic. Charles told himself that he belonged to the latter class and smothered a corroborating belch.

The motive of the present day's party was the launching of a first novel, and the press, book sellers and other interested representatives had been invited to eat, drink and make merry in its honour. They were always being invited to the Moonbeam Room or the Persian Room or this, that or other Room to honour something and knew what was expected of them in return.

A man from the publisher's publicity department hovered attentively around Charles, wondering if his attention was a waste of time. *Culture and Critic* rarely gave good reviews to anyone or anything. Even its faintest praise was made more damnable by an inevitable sting in the tail. Intellectual smearing was Athol Sefton's policy, and as he was proprietor, publisher and editor in chief, there was little Charles could do in return for the martinis and the canapés.

Culture and Critic was a small but influential quarterly, the main office of which was situated in Sydney. It ran a few world syndicated articles and commentaries dealing with music, art and literature, but its main concern was the local artistic scene. With the aid of a secretary, a broken-down journalist and frequent abusive wires, letters and phone calls from Athol, Charles looked after the Melbourne office. The only section in the magazine where he was allowed carte blanche was the detective story review. He was a peaceable young man and this salve to his self-respect evidently enabled him to put up with the tantrums of his uncle by marriage.

Catching sight of Charles across the crowded, smoke-misted room, Margot Stainsbury gave a little shriek of recognition, excused herself ruthlessly to her companion, a dark and dour young man in crumpled corduroy trousers, and began to weave her lovely synthetic body through the drinking groups. Several tired businessmen looked at her with prawn-eyed expectancy, but although she automatically flashed her twenty-guinea-a-shot smile at them, she kept on to the place where Charles was listening to the publisher's representative expounding on the book of the year.

"Darling!" she shrieked again, and flung butterfly arms around his neck, lifting up out of the two suede straps and pencil-like heels which constituted her shoes.

Charles had not seen Margot for nearly a year, at which time he had been brought to the sudden and shattering realisation that she was the sort of girl you only took out to dine and dance.

"Oh—hello!" he said feebly. "What are you doing here?"

She shone a perfunctory smile on his companion, then linked arms affectionately. "Oh, you know me—always around. Angel, I can't tell you how relieved I am to see you. There's something most frightfully important I want to tell you."

The publicity man chivalrously, though reluctantly, began to edge away. He felt *Culture and Critic* owed him something. With a clatter of chunky costume jewellery, Margot put out a restraining hand. "Oh, please don't go. You will make me feel dreadful. I'm sure I am breaking up some most frightfully important discussion. Chas and I can talk later, can't we, dear?"

"It's probably a toss-up which is of more frightful importance, so let's stick to neutral ground," said Charles and introduced them.

"How do you do, Miss Stainsbury. Haven't I see—?"

"Of course you've seen her before," interrupted Charles, with a touch of derision. "Miss Stainsbury is the most sought-after model in the country. Here is the face that launches a thousand sales."

"Oh, Chas!" Margot fluttered her lids demurely. Then, because the publicity man wasn't, as she had first thought, a member of the press and showed an inclination to hover like an unwanted dog after a desultory pat, she said plaintively, "Do you know, I've hardly had one drink yet."

Charles, remembering being the humiliated victim of this gambit of hers, remained unmoved. Slavering happily, the publicity man plunged away to the bar to do Margot's bidding.

"And you round off the trick by moving to another part of the room," said Charles, guiding her through the crowds.

"You didn't mind, darling? He looked the type to cling. Such odd people one has to meet at cocktail parties. You weren't actually talking about anything frightfully important, were you, Charles?"

"He thought so, but not frightfully. He wants Athol to let me write some nice things about the novel that overgrown schoolboy in the corner there has written."

Margot made a parade platform swivel, and surveyed the author with an expertly dispassionate eye. "Is he the cause of all this?"

"Unwittingly, poor fellow! Which reminds me—what are you doing in this commercially erudite company? Not your usual venue if I might say so?"

Her large eyes widened reproachfully, threatening to eclipse the rest of her wholly enchanting face. "I can get by anywhere, so don't act as though you're not pleased to see me. Don't I always read Athol's nasty bits about the latest novels? Oh, and yours too, darling—though I can't understand why you must get so intense about murders and blunt weapons and things."

"The detective story is just as much an artistic expression—" began Charles defensively.

"You see what I mean, dear?" she interrupted kindly. "So boring when you become earnest. Now Athol is never boring, though I agree he can be an absolute beast sometimes. Do you know, Chas, it took me all my time to get him to take me to lunch at Manonetta's last week? He wanted to go to some ghastly out-of-the-way spot, but as I pointed out to him, I can't afford not to be seen. And even when I got him to Manonetta's," her voice rose incredulously, "he absolutely insisted upon a side table. I might just as well have been wearing something off the peg. Don't you agree that was brutish of him?"

"Oh, quite! So you've seen Athol recently. How was he?"

"Darling, I'm just telling you. Do pay attention. A side table at Manonetta's. What I mean to say is—you know Athol! And it can't be just because of his wife's death. I know she was your aunt, Chas, but did you ever see such a drear? Anyway, she's been dead for months now."

Charles thought of his late aunt, whom he was reputed to have resembled, and protested.

"Oh darling, she was! An out-and-out drear. How did Athol come to marry her, even though she did have money? By the way, I trust she did the decent thing by our Charles."

"No, she didn't—at least, not to the extent of your eyeing me in that calculating way, Margot. Athol would be your better bet."

"At the moment Athol is not very impressionable material."

"That's unusual—both for him and for you. Losing your grip, Margot?"

Her eyes flashed momentarily. "Unusual! That's just what I'm telling you, Chas, but you don't seem the least concerned."

"Maybe if I knew what you were talking about I could be concerned. I do wish you would be more concise. Athol is unusual, is that it? But isn't he always?"

"He's not being unusually unusual," she said, with a gesture of impatience. "And he's not pining away after your aunt. Who would? He seems to me to be—well, I know you will just scoff—frightened."

"Athol? Nonsense!"

She gave a little shiver. "Haunted!"

"That's even greater rubbish. I was speaking to him on the phone only this morning. He sounded just the same."

"Yes, haunted is about the right word," Margot nodded in agreement with herself. "We were talking about ghosts too."

"Ghosts? Oh, now, look here—"

"It was after he came back from the telephone. But I'd already noticed how changed he was. We were having claret with our lunch, and do you know it was the first wine the waiter offered? Athol, who likes to make a thing about tasting and sending waiters scurrying! Now, do you understand, Chas?"

"What about the phone call?" asked Charles stolidly.

"Someone called him—just as they were making our Suzettes. Aren't people inconsiderate? But Athol went at once, which is odd too when one comes to think of it. When he came back he ordered a whisky and soda. After all that claret and he never drinks spirits before evening as a rule. Of course, I could see that he was most frightfully shaken about something."

Charles frowned. He could think of only one reason for Athol's alleged change in demeanour—financial anxiety; though it had never seemed to worry him before this. *Culture and Critic* had never been inaugurated as a money-spinning venture. An astringent influence in an uncultured society was the way Athol always referred to it. With its limited circulation and meagre advertisements, it just paid for itself, any lapses from monetary grace being covered by Athol's small private resources and his wife's larger ones. Perhaps the terms of the late Mrs Sefton's will contained some hindrance to this admirable scheme which she had been persuaded against carrying out in life. She had been a semi-invalid for as long as Charles could remember and Athol was capable of making even the strongest woman do what he wanted.

"It was then," Margot was saying in a trilling voice, "that he asked—half-jokingly, of course—if I believed in ghosts. So you understand why I said haunted, Chas?"

"No, I'm afraid I don't. However, Athol is coming down in a day or so. I'll probably learn what the trouble is then—if there is anything and you haven't made all this up, Margot. He wants me to go bush with him—shooting ducks."

"Are you really, darling? How odd! So am I. See that perfectly sweet boy over there? His father runs a hotel at some damn-awful place called Dunbavin. That wouldn't be where you and Athol are going?"

"None other. The Duck and Dog."

"How marvellous to think I won't be leaving civilisation behind altogether. I must go back to Jerry—he gets so jealous, poor pet! If that man ever comes back with my drink, you have it to fortify yourself for Athol. He spoke about you quite savagely after the ghosts."

He watched her rejoin the glowering young man in the velvet trousers. He felt a touch of pity for him. Margot could be quite ruthless.

III

'With a tender smile, Lawrence took Estella in his arms. Her lovely face, framed in a cloudy mist of tulle, looked up at him trustingly. "My darling," he whispered adoringly. "Mine at last".'

Heaving a sigh, Adelaide drew a bold line under the final words of her story and moved her dreamy gaze to the window. The view was not a prepossessing one; a blank brick wall of the next house of the terrace and a flutter of washing hanging on an improvised clothes-line. A slit of sky between the two roofs of rotting slates was the only possible redeeming feature, but Adelaide's vision was turned inwards on the white satin of Estella's wedding gown and Lawrence's handsome face and athletic figure.

The boarding house where the Dougalls resided was perhaps the most sordid and depressing of all they had endured over the past few years. They had been there for six months now, economizing in preparation for their annual migration to the Duck and Dog.

Retirement and the end of the British Raj in India had coincided for Major Dougall. Instead of returning to England, he had decided to settle in Australia, bringing with him his wife and daughter. The army had been the only life he had ever known, and while he had enjoyed every moment of it, his career had been but a modest one. It was not to be expected then that his civilian career would be in any way brilliant. Gullible and short-sighted in investing his small capital, it soon became a failure, and the Dougalls found themselves moving from hotel to flat and on down the scale to a succession of dingy boarding houses as the Major's income shrank.

Years of easy living and the rigid social code of Anglo-Indians had left Mrs Dougall incapable of adjusting herself to a new and cruder life. She clung to the old standards by building a protecting wall of memories of the halcyon Indian years between herself and the sordid realities of the present, behaving, speaking, thinking and even dressing precisely as she had done then. Being a strong-minded woman, she succeeded in bolstering up the Major's flagging morale, so that he almost completely joined her in the happy self-deception. Without her, no doubt, he would have long since pressed his old service revolver to his highly coloured forehead.

Their daughter, Adelaide, however, floated half-way between fast-fading memories of life in Simla and the present. At first, she had made an effort to help the family finances. Against her parents' wishes, who could not realise the need to earn a living, she had tried a commercial course of typing and shorthand. But, unable to master either art and helped on by her mother's disapproval, she had soon given up. In the intervening years, she had picked up a little money by baby-sitting or taking a surreptitious job in a shop during the sales. She was still as immature and diffident as the eager, shy girl who had dispensed tea to the subalterns of her father's regiment on her mother's At Home day. She, too, lived on memories. These included a short-lived, barely developed romance with a junior officer, which had been squashed by Mrs Dougall on the discovery that the young man's father was in trade.

Since then, Adelaide had fallen in love hopelessly numerous times. There was the doctor who had attended her when she had jaundice, a total stranger who had travelled regularly on the same train with her during the summer sales week. She enjoyed the hopeless loves, luxuriating in her nightly wet pillow, but when a fellow-boarder at one of their places of abode showed signs of reciprocation to the extent of trying to enter her room one night, she was immeasurably shocked.

The short stories she wrote in secret, but never submitted for publication for fear of rejection, were sweetly romantic tales invariably ending at the engagement of the handsome hero and heroine—or at the most with the wedding reception and a detailed description of the wedding gown. Sex was some dark, secret thing that she kept on the other side of the wall, like her mother and father kept the harsh world at bay. She always skipped the frank passages in books and averted her eyes carefully whenever she saw a pregnant woman. Such things had nothing to do with Adelaide's ideas of love, and even if they did come to her mind in hot unguarded moments, they were still not to be connected with—with Him.

Her new love, which she had nursed for eighteen months now, was more hopeless than any she had ever cherished before. Her masochism was heightened by the fact that the man was married. She had based a story on her plight, in which an accomplished and charming girl (which was how Adelaide sometimes dreamed herself to be instead of plain, spinsterish and inarticulate) falls in love with a distinguished and learned man some years her senior (which was how He appeared in her eyes), unhappily married to an invalid, querulous wife incapable of sharing his interests (which was how Adelaide imagined His wife to be). The poignant renunciation scene between the would-be lovers still moved her whenever she re-read the story.

Sitting at the window of her musty little bedroom, Adelaide's heart suddenly beat fast under her flattened bosom. A flush spread over her thin, sallow face as she thought of how that story might even yet come true—but with a changed and happy ending. For the first time in her life, she found herself wanting to face reality.

The change had taken place suddenly. They had been at breakfast, Mrs Dougall opening the single letter on her plate with the air of one about to deal with a pile of social invitations, and the Major with his red face and bristling white moustache hidden behind the more conservative of the morning papers. In his high, strangulated voice, which always sounded as though his uvula was in the way of his larynx, Major Dougall had said, "I see that fellah has lost his wife. Died—um—let's see the date—two days ago."

Adelaide looked up quickly from the unappetising rissoles on her plate. 'That fellah' could only be one person. Athol Sefton. Her father had harkened back to him several times during the year, making plain his dislike which was like a nagging tooth to be eased only by being clenched. When her father had finished with the paper, she took it up to her room. There was no doubt at all as to who it was. His querulous, invalid wife was dead. He was free!

"Free at last!" whispered Adelaide exultantly. Suddenly the wife seemed to have been the only obstacle in the way of her happiness.

From that moment on, Adelaide Dougall concentrated on an imaginary situation which to her had now become real. Each word and glance that he had ever given her was pondered upon and built up into occasions of deep significance. Their parting and the past months of separation had been as intolerable to him as they had been to her—of that she became convinced. She even looked for word from him, but when no letter came she told herself that, of course, it would not be proper for him to get in touch with her yet.

But that did not stop her from raking the crowded city streets and passing to and fro in front of the hotel where she knew he stayed when he was in Melbourne. But, of course, he intended waiting until they met again at their first place of meeting—the Duck and Dog at Dunbavin. It was the sort of romantic gesture that she could appreciate, and she began to mark off the dates on her calendar.

Thus, as the weeks went by and became days, Adelaide worked herself up to a feverish, erotic pitch which was as pitiful as it was dangerous.

IV

I should have checked in to a larger hotel, thought Jeffrey. Here I stick out like a sore thumb. Maybe if I talked like some of these Aussies—"Oi'm stying at the Hotel Broight," he essayed aloud, and made a derisive sound.

'Stying' is just about it, he thought, staring at the dirty curtains which shrouded dirtier windows overlooking the rubbish-littered backyard of the hotel. Lying on the bed, cradling a glass of beer on his chest, he remembered the way the chambermaid had said, "You're an American, aren't you? Just fancy!" as though he was someone from Mars.

Hell, didn't they remember the Yanks here? It wasn't so long ago. Maybe folks' memories are short when they know they should be grateful. It didn't seem that long ago to him since they had been here. Camp Pell, they had called it. He had taken a ride out there, just for old times' sake, to have a look at it—to remember himself as a kid in olive drab, sweating it out in the South Pacific Theatre. The cab driver had asked him if he had ever come up against that American soldier who murdered those three women.

Jeffrey's body grew taut and his fingers suddenly clenched on the glass. He raised his head and, finishing the beer, set the glass on the bed table which already had a film of dust on it before the ashtray overflowed with his own cigarette ends. He lay back again, his hands under his head and a wry grin on his lips. That's a word you'll have to get used to, son, he told himself.

'But they won't get me like they got Leonski—I'm not a psychopathic strangler. There's a difference between murdering for the hell of it and—the bastard, the dirty rotten bastard!' he thought suddenly, burning up.

Funny how the years hadn't minimised his fury or mellowed his bitterness. He had carried the injury with him all this time, so that he felt almost that he had grown up with it—that it was as much a part of him and as familiar as his own body. He always knew that one day he would come back to do what he had sworn to do on that reeking, sweltering atoll somewhere in the Pacific where he had received the news. Instinctively his hand crept to his inside coat pocket, encountering first the holster where his Luger lay snug against his side, then the old shagreen wallet where he had kept the letter from that moment outside the master-sergeant's palm-thatched hut. Return and revenge had been his goal in the same way as other men's goals were to be president of a company or captain of a baseball team. He had worked towards it, preparing himself both physically and mentally.

Sometimes he had tried to fight against inexorable ambition which kept driving him on, telling himself that the years were passing, what did it matter, what had happened to him had happened to other men and would happen again. But still he went on making plans and marking every saved dollar for a special purpose.

A knock at the door caused him to start up tensely. "Are you there, Mr Jeffrey? There's someone to see you."

He guessed who it would be, but still he asked for the name before unlocking the door.

A neatly dressed, middle-aged man, rather like a trusted bank clerk, entered. His small eyes behind bi-focal glasses were both watchful and observant as he was as insistent on checking the American's identity as Jeffrey had been in checking his. "We have to be very careful in our business, Mr Jeffrey," he said, more as a statement of fact than by way of apology.

"Sit down," the other invited, shaking up a cigarette to offer his visitor, "and tell me what you've got for me."

"Thank you, no. I don't care for American cigarettes. Regarding the party you commissioned us to trace," he went on, pulling out a notebook and turning over the pages. "He left Sydney on the eleven thirty plane this morning and is due to arrive any moment now. He is being met by a man called Carmichael who is his nephew by marriage. His wife, just in case it is of interest to you, died a few months ago. So far we can discover no reservation made for him at any hotel. It is my belief that he will be staying with his nephew who has a bachelor flat just outside the city. I have his address with me if you want it.

"From the evening of the 27th—that is, tomorrow—the party has a booking at a hotel in the country some hundred and fifty miles away. The name of this hotel is the Duck and Dog. It is situated near the town of Dunbavin. Your party usually spends the first part of March there every year for the duck-shooting. We are unable to anticipate his movements further," the little man concluded, as though defying anyone else to be able.

But I can, thought the American exultantly. Shooting ducks, huh? I know one who is a dead duck right now.

The private enquiry agent went on. "We were uncertain of your precise wishes, Mr Jeffrey, but following the general tone of your instructions we took the chance on booking you in at the same hotel. I trust we acted correctly?"

"Fine!" said Jeffrey, trying to keep the note of reckless triumph out of his voice. The whole business was turning out better than if he had planned it.

The agent gave a little deprecatory cough. "Naturally we do not enquire into our clients' intentions, or the outcome of the work they ask us to undertake—" he paused, his small shrewd eyes on the American's face.

The other said sharply, "Yes, go on!"

After a pause, the agent said, "Very often after much careful and discreet work on our part, our clients undo it all by behaving foolishly."

Jeffrey's facial muscles felt stiff as he tried to grin easily. "What are you getting at?"

"Just a little advice, if you don't think it out of order. Is it your intention, now that we have finished our commission on your behalf, to continue to keep your party under observation?"

Jeffrey lit another cigarette. His fingers were trembling slightly. "Could be," he replied. "But I thought you said you started minding your own business at this point."

"Sometimes the point is marginal. In your case I feel compelled to advise you to keep in part with your environment. In other words, Mr Jeffrey, if you wish to continue—let us say anonymously—you had better go to the Duck and Dog prepared and equipped to shoot ducks."

The American coughed over his cigarette as a laugh of relief caught him unawares. "Thanks for the tip. It would be sticking my neck way out if I didn't dress and act the part."

The agent looked gratified, then shook his head. "It is not so much acting and dressing. I'm afraid the fact that you are an

American will make you stand out, so to speak, in the district you intend to visit. The point is, can you shoot?"

His client laughed again. "Sure I can shoot. They taught us to do that sort of thing back in '42."

"Ah yes, quite! War is a terrible thing," said the agent with the air of announcing a profound and original truth. "But there is, I believe, a difference between shooting game and—ah—sniping at the enemy. What you need is a shotgun. In order to preserve your anonymity I suggest your purchasing one before you leave town."

"You're being most considerate," murmured Jeffrey.

Again the little man looked pleased. "Don't mention it. It's just that I do like a job to be tucked in on all corners, so to speak. Now here is the name of a reliable gunsmith. All the best sportsmen go there, I believe."

"Why, thanks a lot—"

"You're welcome. It is our aim to give our clients every possible service in order to achieve their objectives—short of murder, of course." He tittered lightly as he drew out a folded slip of paper. "Now, if you are quite satisfied, Mr Jeffrey, there is just the little matter of our account."

"I'll settle up right away," said the American jerkily, turning away from him to take out his wallet.

Money and receipt were exchanged. Then the agent packed up his briefcase and went to the door. "Well, goodbye, Mr Jeffrey—and good luck. I hope you have an enjoyable time shooting ducks."

V

"Dunbavin!" said Andrew, easing the utility over one of the many bumps of the rough country road. "Look it up on the map, will you, darling? I believe the F. and G. recommend it too."

Frances unwrapped the map and spread it over her knees, bending forward to hide the small tolerant smile that women smile when they think they know how to manage their men.

Their unconventional honeymoon had started off in New South Wales shooting marauding kangaroos, on which an open season had been declared. Then on further south, where they had tried their luck with the wild pigs that roamed about the Murrumbidgee. Late February found them crossing the Murray into Victoria, where duck-shooting was the next item on Andrew's list.

He slipped a sudden arm about his wife's shoulders. Life was good. Frankie was a grand wife. He had enjoyed teaching her how to shoot, marvelling at her occasional fluke, for he maintained it needed years of practise to become a really accomplished shot. Perhaps he enjoyed her ineptitude even more.

Then there were the warm twilights when they made camp just where they fancied, and Frances squatted over the fire he had lighted cooking kangaroo steak or a rabbit stew, her face intent and shadowy in the firelight. His arm tightened so that she was pulled sideways against him as he thought of the nights hazy with stars when they lay rolled in blankets, Frances small and silent in his arms.

"Look out, Andy!" Frances protested, wriggling free. "You're making me tear the map."

"To hell with the map," he replied, and the truck swerved crazily as he gave her a swift kiss. "Happy?"

"Of course. Look, if we follow this road it seems to lead to the main highway to Dunbavin."

"Okay—we're off to see Dunbavin, Dunbavin the place for ducks!" he sang, leaning forward and putting both hands at the top of the wheel. "You're really happy, Frankie? Like being married to me?"

"Of course," she said again, sounding surprised. "What silly questions you ask, darling!"

Somehow he felt oddly comforted when she called him that. She had a lovely voice, Frankie had, when she chose to put expression into it—sort of warm and husky. It must be all the amateur acting she did at home. Everyone used to say that she ought to try her luck in Sydney—study for the stage or try television audition, perhaps go abroad. He was damned thankful she hadn't.

"Look!" he said suddenly, slowing the utility and lifting one hand to point. "They know we're coming. They're up to welcome us."

A slow-moving formation of ducks appeared in the sky ahead. They seemed to hang immobile before dropping down behind a clump of low trees which hid a lagoon. "They are a good omen," said Frances and put her hand into his.

Just as the term of endearment had pleased him, so the spontaneous gesture of affection brought a surge of something like gratitude. Impulsively he said, "This pub—the Duck and Dog—what say we put up there for a night or two? I bet you've had enough sleeping in the open. What about a change from roughing it?"

"But Andy, we'd never get in. They're certain to be full up and the expense—"

Andrew was himself again, confident and masterful. "Bet you anything you like I can get us in and hang the expense. Aren't we on our honeymoon?"

"There is no harm in trying, I suppose," she returned doubtfully. "And it would be nice to eat a meal someone else has cooked for a change."

"I've no complaints to make about the present cook. We'll enquire where this joint is when we get to Dunbavin."

He pressed the car forward over the corrugated road.

"Andy, I'm sure it must be somewhere near here. We're coming to the main highway and the map says it is this side of the town."

They glided on to the smooth bitumen. "That's a relief," said Andrew. "Hullo! Looks like one of the natives ahead. We'll stop and see if they talk the same language south of the border."

It was Wilson, the first guest at Ellis Bryce's hotel.

"Good-day there!" greeted Andrew. "Can you tell us where to find a pub called the Duck and Dog?"

Wilson struggled with his Adam's apple, his eyes fixed with intense concentration on the car's number plate. "There's a t-t-turn—" and he pointed further along.

"A turning a bit on?" Andrew queried, unconsciously imitating Ellis. "Left or right?"

"L—l—"

"Left, is it? Thanks, mate. Much obliged." He drew his head in and put the car into gear, giving Frances a broad wink. Wilson with his solemn face and painful stammer was a terrific figure of fun to him. An inarticulate sound made him turn back. "You were saying?"

Wilson made a stupendous effort and left out the extraneous words people with impediments will try to use. "Duck-shooting?"

"That's so," returned Andrew, surprised at the sudden clarity. "The wife and I want to put up at the pub for a night or two. We heard there was good sport round these parts."

Wilson screwed his head round and blinked in a puzzled fashion at Frances. Maintaining his telegraphic style of elocution, he asked, "Name, Morton?"

"Turner's the name. But what's that to do with you?"

The other flapped his hands around for a moment. "F-full-up," he brought out at last.

"There you are, Andy," said Frances.

"You the proprietor?" Andrew asked Wilson, who shook his head. "Then how do you know they're full up? The season doesn't open until Monday. Oh, a guest, huh! Well, maybe we'll go along and enquire just the same. Be seeing you, sport!"

He tilted his jaw and there was a determined look in his eyes as they came to a narrow dirt road little better than a cart track. A sagging signpost, which Ellis Bryce had had erected in the first flush of inspiration, bore the direction PRIVATE ROAD: DUCK AND DOG INN. He put the car into second as it made its first climb for many miles. "I'm not going to let a little twerp like that put me off. Nosey sort of bloke, wasn't he?"

Presently the hotel came into view—a sturdy two-storied building of stone with sprawling additions of sun-blistered weatherboard clinging about it like parasitic growths.

"Well, this is it! Stay where you are and keep your fingers crossed, honey."

"Good hunting, Mr Fixit," Frances returned brightly. She watched him stride confidently to the open door which was set in the centre of the building between two beds of colourful geraniums. Presently a worried-looking woman with wispy untidy hair and dressed in an overall appeared. Andrew put one hand on his hip and stamped his feet about as he spoke to her, which was how he always stood when he was being aggressive and not quite sure of himself.

The woman put a hand up to her hair as though making sure it was still untidy, and glanced vaguely in the direction of the utility as she listened. Presently she interrupted the barrage and disappeared into the house. With a wink and a thumbs-up sign at Frances, Andrew followed.

A few minutes later, he emerged, grinning triumphantly. "Okay, Frankie! I've made it. Hop out and I'll get our stuff."

"Andy, you're marvellous! However did you do it?"

"Gift of the gab mostly. Though there was a room booked and the people haven't turned up. Had a telly or something from them only this morning. So balls to that stuttering little chap we met. Will his face be red when he sees us!"

PART TWO

Murder and Motives

I

The flat-bottomed old boat rocked dangerously as Athol Sefton staggered, gave an odd little choking cough, then sagged slowly across the gunwhale. His twelve-gauge double-barrelled Greenet sank into the muddy water, his hand trailing limply after it.

The two explosions had sounded almost simultaneously. Out of the beat of wings and noises of alarm above the lagoon, a chestnut-breasted teal, caught in flight, had dropped a hundred yards away. It lay floating in eddying circles with its neck askew. Wimpey, one of the spaniels from the Duck and Dog, went out to it almost as soon as it hit the water.

Charles Carmichael, sitting in the stern of the boat, stared incredulously at the humped figure of his uncle leaning over the side—the result of the second shot. The bright stain spreading over Athol's shooting jacket held his bemused gaze.

Presently all became still again. The birds had made off and the boat stopped its crazy movement. The spaniel bitch came swimming back with the dead bird in her jaw. She nosed around the limp, trailing hand and made whining sounds. Receiving no response, she swam to Charles. He released the bird and flung it distastefully on the bottom of the boat. Then he climbed along the tilted boat and with much effort managed to turn the body over. Athol's eyes were open and glazing fast. There was a frothy stain on his lips and the blood on his jacket was starting to congeal. He had been shot under Charles's gaze, standing up to fire at the ducks.

Cautiously, Charles stood upright so that he was head and shoulders over the thicket of reeds into which they had pushed the boat. He gave an apprehensive look around, ready to duck for cover, but apart from the birds settling on the further end of the lagoon, there was no sign of movement. The scene was as desolate and uninviting in his eyes as when, less than an hour earlier, feeling cold, sleepy and irritable, he had crept with Athol through the low-lying scrub with a gun under his arm. He had not seen the sense of getting up at an ungodly hour just to bring down a few ducks before anyone else, but Athol had insisted upon his companionship.

Now look what has happened, thought Charles—so staggered by the turn of events that he felt a puerile indignation.

In spite of his absorption in fictional crime, an interest amounting almost to an intellectual passion, it was to come to him only slowly that the shot which had killed Athol had not been the accidental firing of a careless gunman, but the well-aimed shot of a marksman.

Leaving the boat wedged in the reeds, he made his way across the marshy ground to the track which led to the road. From there he jog-trotted the mile and a half back to the Duck and Dog.

The hotel was in the depths of early Sunday silence, the rising sun striking the mellow old stone. He went through the empty ground floor, past the stairs, to a door which led to one of the weatherboard annexes. Ellis Bryce had his bedroom there, because he did not see the point of climbing up and down stairs any more than being an unnecessary distance from the bar.

He came to the door in pyjamas, yawning and stretching. "Ah—good morning, Mr Carmichael! I won't ask what I can do for you because I never do anything for anyone—least of all at this hour. In fact, I leave all complaints to my sister, Grace."

"I don't know if you will regard it in the nature of a complaint," said Charles light-headedly, "but my uncle is dead."

Ellis Bryce dropped his arms slowly and his brows went up. "Dear, dear! Poor Athol! I'm sorry to hear that. Heart, I suppose.

I must say I thought he looked and behaved muchly the same last night—how the dear fellow loved to churn the party up—but Shelagh mentioned something about his not looking so well. You might not know my daughter properly yet, Mr Carmichael, but what she says is always accurate. A most efficient girl!"

"Most," agreed Charles, who had tried to make headway with Shelagh and knew Ellis was pricking him gently. "But this time she is wrong. My uncle was shot though the chest."

Ellis's imperturbability was shaken, but after a pause he said, "What a bad shot you must be! Or was it with intent?"

Charles gaped at him, then exclaimed in shocked accents, "What the devil—"

"Oh, pray forgive me," said Ellis, waving an airy hand. "I always endeavour to view life—and death—light-heartedly first thing in the morning. Was it the pukka sahib who shot him? Or the spurned Adelaide? 'Hell hath no fury as a woman scorned'. Dear me, how your news has affected me! Never have I sunk so far as to quote—and such a cliché—at this hour."

"I would be obliged if you would stop being facetious about a very serious matter," said Charles stiffly.

"My apologies again. However, to maintain the revolting flow which seems to have attacked me, many a true word is spoken in jest."

"There are some subjects one does not jest about," said Charles angrily. "I came to you because—"

"What a remark from one who reviews detective stories so ably and wittily," interrupted Ellis, bent on being infuriating. "I always say your mordant comments are the one thing worth reading in Athol's depressingly esoteric periodical. Perhaps an enraged author shot Athol by mistake for you. Do let me know the results of your cogitations on this matter later. Now I must go back to bed."

"Oh no, you don't," said Charles, putting his foot in the door. "What do you advise I should do about Athol?"

Ellis looked pained. "My dear Mr Carmichael, I never give advice.

I have already exerted myself enough for your benefit—without a doubt the poor unpleasant fellow was murdered. I refuse to have my brain picked further. However, as you seem nonplussed, I suggest the mundane ritual of burial should come next—or cremation. I understand your late Aunt Paula enjoyed a final combustion. However much one disliked him in life, one must respect Athol's last wishes."

There was a brisk tap of feet coming down the stairs, and Ellis cocked his head. "Ah—my daughter Shelagh—so efficient at handling mundane situations. I recommend you to her."

Charles turned in relief as the girl came down the passage. She was dressed in a tailored skirt and a spotless white blouse, her face and hair attractive and neat. She was on her way to the kitchen to start the breakfast before her aunt Grace got there.

"Shelagh, my dear, Athol Sefton has been shot and Mr Carmichael wants to know what to do next. What do you suggest?"

The girl glanced from one to the other sharply. "Shot? Is he badly hurt?"

"Dead," said Charles, surprised at the baldness of his own reply. It was extraordinary to realise that Athol was no longer alive. "We were over at that lagoon about a mile from here. He had just stood up and had actually fired when some fool of a person on the other side shot without looking."

"You had no business being out at all," said Shelagh reprovingly, as though Athol had received his just deserts for disobedience. "The season does not open until tomorrow."

"You must tell that to the person whose shot killed Athol," rejoined Charles, nettled. "In the meantime I would like some practical advice."

"You're asking just the right person, my boy," said Ellis, clapping him on the shoulder. "A very practical girl, my daughter. But if there is one thing I abominate more than being asked advice, it is listening to someone else give it. So excuse me if I retire."

"With pleasure and much relief," said Charles grimly.

"You had better ring Sergeant Motherwell at Dunbavin," said Shelagh and led the way to the phone in the gunroom. "And Dr Spenser too. I'll get the number for you."

Charles muttered a word of thanks and listened to her deal kindly but firmly with the moronic telephonist in the town.

"Father being trying?" she enquired calmly, as they waited for the police station to answer.

"Very," replied Charles in heartfelt accents. "First of all he suggested I had shot Athol—then that he had been murdered possibly in mistake for me."

She looked him over dispassionately. "I'm sure no one would want to murder you."

"That sounds something between a compliment and an insult."

She made as though to say something more when the phone was answered. "Mrs Motherwell? Is Tom there? Shelagh Bryce speaking."

"What were you going to say?" asked Charles, taking the receiver she held out to him.

"Only that I can imagine there could be people who might have liked to murder Athol," she announced coolly.

"That is a matter for the police to decide," said Charles guardedly.

He listened to the approach of heavy deliberate footsteps, the noise of the phone being lifted, then breathing to match the tread. "Hullo, there!" he said impatiently.

"Now then, what's all this about?" asked a ponderous voice. Charles's worst fears were aroused as he wriggled his toes in revulsion at the timeworn phrase. "I was told Miss Bryce wanted me."

"My name is Carmichael. Miss Bryce told me to call you. I want to report a—an accident. My uncle, Athol Sefton, has been shot dead."

There was a pause while Charles listened to the breathing growing heavier. "Did you hear what I said?"

"I heard," said the voice, aggrieved. "I'm just writing down particulars. Hey, mother! Have you got another pencil? This one's broken." There was a gabble in the background, and the sergeant said aside, "Out at the Duck and Dog. That Mr Sefton has been killed."

There were more expostulatory words in the background. Charles thought he caught something about 'no loss, I'm sure', and cut in impatiently, "Keep particulars for when you see me. You had better come out here as quickly as you can." He rang off, remarking bitterly, "Until now I always thought doltish policemen figments of authors' imagination."

A sudden twinkle of sympathy in Shelagh's eyes made him feel that it might be worthwhile persevering with her after all.

She took the phone up again. "Maisie, get me two-four, please. Yes, the doctor's house." She put her hand over the mouthpiece. "Your uncle seemed different from the last time he was here. Had he not been well?"

"He was being plagued by anonymous telephone calls and letters."

"How unpleasant! What were they about?"

"He wouldn't tell me, but I think he might have been taking them seriously. I can't understand why he didn't report the matter to the police. He travelled under another name on the flight from Sydney, and when I met him at Melbourne airport, he was all huddled up in an overcoat and wearing dark glasses. Not that the disguise did much good. A note had been left for him at the gunsmith in Melbourne when he bought his Greenet."

"But you don't know what was in it? How strange not to confide in you."

"There was a certain understanding between us, but never much love lost. A stranger matter was his insistence on spending the night at my flat instead of going to a hotel. I had the impression he wanted me under his eye, which was also his reason for dragging me up to this damn-awful place—as Margot Stainsbury dubbed your home town. At the moment I'm inclined to agree with her."

Shelagh's face became chilly and she turned to deal with the high, quacking voice which came through the wire. Charles remembered the polite sparring match between her and Margot, who had arrived at the Duck and Dog accompanied by Jerry Bryce, the glowering young man of the cocktail party. Her brother's latest infatuation pleased her no more than the others had. Athol had been quick to exploit the situation, exchanging slightly erotic banter with Margot both to annoy Shelagh and to arouse Jerry's jealousy. But it had been Charles's impression that Margot was trying to capture his more serious attention. In fact, Athol had said, maliciously frank, "I believe the woman wants me to marry her." Margot had countered swiftly, "Darling Athol, what an incredible notion! You'd make a perfectly poisonous husband, as I am sure poor Paula discovered."

Young Bryce was one of those unfortunate persons who can never become angry without becoming inarticulate as well. Athol had played him like a fish on his verbal line, throwing practised taunts with the urbanity of one who never allows his emotions to get the better of his intellect.

What a jolly night we had, reflected Charles. The only one who had appeared to remain impervious had been Ellis Bryce. Major and Mrs Dougall had taken umbrage at the first opportunity, while their daughter, Adelaide, who had been unfortunate enough to overhear some humiliating remarks Athol had passed on her, had spent the evening staring at nothing with blank, piteous eyes. The American, Harris Jeffrey, had kept his fists in a perpetually clenched state, as Athol entertained the company with his views on the morals, culture and character of all Americans. Of the other guests, Wilson was subtly mocked to his twitching unhappy face, and the young honeymooners, who had tried to take Athol in the best guesthouse spirit, had soon retreated, wounded and bewildered.

Shelagh, having successfully baulked Mrs Spenser's well-known curiosity, rang off. Charles said to her, "Do you know what all this reminds me of? One of those detective stories about an ill-assorted group weekending at a country house. I think everyone was about ripe for murder by the time Athol had finished last night."

"Don't be absurd!" she said sharply. "You are to go and wait at the main road. Dr Spenser is picking Sergeant Motherwell up and will meet you there."

"Won't you come too? I need you to keep my imagination at bay."

She shook her head and went to the door. "What happens now is not my affair. Besides, I must get the breakfast started. There's Aunt Grace coming down now."

Charles scowled after her. She made perseverance seem an impossible task.

II

"Absolutely no doubt at all," pronounced Dr Spenser.

"I entirely concur," proclaimed Sergeant Motherwell.

Charles, who had already summed them up as a pair of fools, one pompous and the other sycophantic, protested against their verdict of accidental death. During the time they had taken to move Athol from the lagoon boat to the road, he had been occupied by the disturbing thought that Ellis's lighthearted suggestion of murder might not be so ludicrous after all.

"But what about the bullet?" he asked.

Dr Spenser regarded him in a lofty professional manner. "What about the bullet?" he queried. He made a habit of making a question of a question. It made him sound omniscient and usually abashed the enquirer.

"You don't fire bullets at ducks," said Charles defensively.

"My dear fellow, these amateurs use anything—rifles, repeaters, pistols—but anything at all. Every season there is some fatality or other like this. We had one in this district only two years ago, am I not right, Tom?"

The policeman nodded solemnly. "That is correct, Doctor. It was a near thing to having the chap up for manslaughter."

"But this isn't manslaughter," said Charles loudly. "It's murder."

The doctor looked him over as coldly as though he had been requested to perform an illegal operation. "My good fellow, that's an appalling statement to make. I can only presume that the natural sorrow you are feeling has caused the indiscretion."

"Indiscretion be damned!" Charles retorted. "Natural sorrow likewise. I never felt any personal regard for Athol in my life—and least of all now seeing the mess he has left for me to clear up. So you can cut out any emotion from my attitude. But I say he was murdered and if you two would only do your job properly—"

"Now, wait a minute," interrupted Motherwell, drawing himself up like an inflated frog. "We are prepared to make allowances for natural—um—shock, shall we say? But you must not talk like that, you know, Mr Carmichael. You can't go making wild statements without the evidence to back them up."

"Well, what of the bullet, to start with?"

"That has already been accounted for," said the policeman with a glance at the doctor.

"Not to my satisfaction, it hasn't," retorted Charles. "Then what about the season not being open until tomorrow? Yes, I know we shouldn't have been out either, but that is beside the point. In fact, had I but known—" He broke off, horrified at the words that had slipped out involuntarily. He always panned mercilessly those emotional mystery stories whose writers belonged to what Mr Ogden Nash referred to as the H.I.B.K. school.

Dr Spenser and the sergeant regarded him with puzzled animosity. "What I mean is," he went on lamely, "it is unlikely that any sportsman would have been out today other than my uncle, who always made a point of breaking rules. Look at Major Dougall—you probably know him as he has been here before—he would not dream of shooting today."

"Just what are you suggesting, Mr Carmichael?"

"That someone guessed that Athol was likely to go shooting ducks this morning, and took the opportunity of no one else being nearby to kill him."

"What nonsense!" said the doctor testily. "Motherwell, it is up to you. I've given you my opinion as a medical man, but yours is the final word."

The policeman said with ponderous dignity, "I can only presume that Mr Carmichael's imagination is running away with him. I shall put in a full report concerning this distressing affair; naturally there will be an inquest. Mr Carmichael need have no fear that this business will not be wound up entirely to the satisfaction of unbiased authority. But such wild talk of murder cannot be condoned. I must request you, sir, not to voice such fantastic beliefs."

"I haven't got that much imagination," said Charles irritably. "Otherwise I would write books instead of reviewing them. And my beliefs are not fantastic but feasible. My uncle had some trouble on his mind. I don't say he realised his life was in danger, but he was a changed man—and what is more I can produce witnesses to back me up in that statement."

There was a pause; then the doctor said thoughtfully, "What sort of books do you review, Mr Carmichael? Ah, yes! You are associated with Mr Sefton in the production called *Culture and Critic*."

"Detective novels," replied Charles defiantly. "But that has nothing to do with the matter in hand."

"Ah," said the policeman, his tone of voice indicating that all was now clear. He lost some of his hostility, and a slightly tolerant gleam came into his eye.

Dr Spenser gave an amused shrug. "My dear fellow, I'm an ardent detective novel fan myself—in fact, I follow your reviews in the choice of my reading matter—but I don't go round applying the principles of fiction to my everyday life."

Motherwell laughed. "Otherwise I'd have to keep my eye on you, Doctor. They say in books that the best persons qualified to commit murder are of the medical profession."

"Mind you," said the doctor, now quite jocular with Charles, as though he were a mental defective to be coaxed into reasonable behaviour, "I don't say I wouldn't like to do so with some of my patients."

"I could name one or two," said the policeman, entering into the spirit of things.

"I can only think," said Charles coldly, "that you do not want to get to the bottom of this affair. Tell me, Doctor, you probably met Athol here some season or other—how did you get on with him?"

Dr Spenser raised supercilious brows. "Yes, I knew him. He consulted me last year about some fibrositis trouble he was having. He was not the type of man to take to, as a rule."

"What you mean is, you disliked him heartily. Don't worry—most people did. But just the same that's very interesting. Tell me again, Doctor," he asked, with deceptive smoothness, "are you a shooter too?"

After a short pause, during which his brows lowered themselves into a frown, Dr Spenser said abruptly, "Yes, as a matter of fact, I am."

"Ah!" said Charles, as the policeman had made the ejaculation.

"Well, I think we have wasted enough time on fruitless discussion," said the doctor briskly, throwing Charles a glance of unbridled dislike. "I'll take Mr Sefton's body back to the surgery for a fuller examination, Motherwell, and write out my report for you. Do you want a lift back to the hotel, Carmichael?"

Charles refused the perfunctory offer stiffly. He waited until the car was out of sight, then made his way through the moist, stunted undergrowth to the lagoon. The chestnut-breasted teal Athol had brought down still lay in the bottom of the boat. He picked it up and stood for a moment, thoughtfully surveying the surrounding countryside. The sun was climbing steadily; what had been grey-green and vague outlines were now sparkling highlights and deep shadows. He could see now that the lagoon deepened into a wide sweep away to the right. Across the water from where Athol had stood upright to take aim was a narrow arm of land covered by low trees. Behind it, not so far distant, was the shape of Campbell's Hill.

Still carrying the bird by the legs, and further encumbered by the guns, Charles skirted the edge of the lagoon and made for the peninsula. It was a trying walk through prickly bush with the ground uncertain under his feet; once or twice he sank ankle-deep in mud. Flies, attracted by the dead bird, tormented him, and he brushed them away irritably.

But when he reached the clump of trees all regret of the unpleasant trip was forgotten in the triumph of his surmise being correct. There were faint marks of footprints between the trees and a particularly clear one near the water's edge, where the quick-drying sun had made a cast of it in mud. A man's shoe, he decided after studying it, with rubber treads on the sole.

III

Back at the Duck and Dog, the guests were just starting breakfast. In the kitchen, Miss Bryce was panting from table to stove to sink, spearing sausages, cracking eggs and swooping down on the electric toaster with cries of triumph as she managed to catch the bread before it incinerated. Shelagh moved in and out of her wild sorties with cool, effortless grace, looking collected and superior as she cut grapefruit into artistic shapes and rolled butter into neat dewy curls.

"Porridge for Major and Mrs Dougall—is your father up yet, Shelagh? I am sure I never knew such a—that American person will probably want orange juice, but he'll have to take grapefruit or lump it—though I'm sure he's a very pleasant man. He certainly took Mr Sefton's nastiness very well last night. Porridge for the Turners. Mr Sefton didn't make much headway there, I noticed. What did he expect when she's on her honeymoon? I thought Mrs Turner managed very well, poor little thing—her husband seemed put out and I don't blame him. I do wish your father wouldn't let Mr Sefton come. Look at the way Jerry went on over that model creature. I do believe he delights in making trouble—just as your father delights in looking on."

"Well, he won't be coming again," said Shelagh, turning to put food at the servery window.

"How are you so certain this is Mr Sefton's last season?"

"Because he's dead," returned Shelagh off-handedly. "Do watch what you're doing—you're dropping porridge on the floor."

"What did you say?" asked Miss Bryce incredulously.

Shelagh took the saucepan from her hand and poured neat islands into the willow-pattern bowls. "Mr Sefton was shot dead while out duck-shooting this morning."

"How do you know this? Does your father—why didn't you tell me before?"

The girl shrugged. "It's nothing to do with us. It happened over at Teal Lagoon. Charles Carmichael was with him and came rushing back to tell Father. I rang up Tom Motherwell and Dr Spenser. I suppose they're out there inspecting the body. There's no need to get agitated about things, Aunt."

Miss Bryce was looking aghast. "Nothing to do with us! I should hope not. Dear, dear—what a dreadful—whatever happened, I wonder?"

"I understand Athol came into someone else's range of fire," said Shelagh, backing through the wing door to the dining room, and leaving her aunt, who could never stop once she started, to address her remarks to the boiling kettle.

"I just loathe firearms—something always goes wrong sooner or later—that man who was killed two years back—and then that boy who tripped over his gun climbing through a fence."

Charles came in as Shelagh was placing porridge on the Dougalls' table. He looked dishevelled and cross, and still carried by the tips of his fingers the duck Athol had shot.

"What do I do with this thing?" he demanded, going up to her.

Major Dougall let drop his table napkin, which he had been holding to protect his worn regimental tie from porridge splashes, and gave a harrumph. "Where the deuce did you get that bird?" he demanded in his strangulated voice.

"Athol shot it," said Charles shortly.

"Just put it in the kitchen," said Shelagh. "Your breakfast is ready if you'll sit down."

"The fellah had no business to go shooting this morning," said Major Dougall, addressing his wife. "What's more that's a—"

"I want a word with you," Charles murmured to Shelagh, following her to the kitchen.

Miss Bryce pounced on him. "Oh, Mr Carmichael, Shelagh told me—I was never so shocked—I suppose you'll be leaving now. Oh, dear, that makes two rooms empty. Ellis never seems to care, but the season is most important to us financially and now Mr Sefton—"

"Then at least you're one person who did not wish Athol dead," Charles cut in suddenly.

Shelagh, who had been pouring water into tea and coffee pots, said quickly. "Here, Aunt! Coffee for the Dougalls, tea for the Turners. You take them—I want to squeeze oranges for Mr Jeffrey."

"I told you so," Miss Bryce said accusingly, taking the tray to the dining room.

"Thanks for getting rid of her," said Charles.

"I don't think you should say things like that to Aunt Grace," returned the girl coldly, "or to anyone else, for that matter."

"Sorry. Blame official obtuseness. That fool of a Motherwell says Athol was shot by accident—some unknown and careless sportsman. Did you ever know such a blithering idiot?" Charles thrust his hands into his pockets and strode restlessly around the kitchen. "Of course that pompous old horse, Spenser, called the tune. Just because something like this happened two years ago, they assume Athol was killed by accident. Can you believe it!"

"Yes, I can," said Shelagh deliberately. "Of course it was an accident if Tom and Dr Spenser say so. The trouble with you is that you are letting your imagination—"

Charles threw out a hand. "Don't! Please don't say that. No one is more anxious than I that Athol's death should be accidental. As well as for reasons of kinship, I have no ambition to figure in a real-life murder case. In fact, the idea fairly revolts me. So just disabuse yourself of the notion that I am savouring this situation academically."

"If that's how you feel," said the girl practically, "then you should be relieved by their opinion."

"I should," he agreed, "but would you stand by when you knew there was more to things than met the eye? Now look, I've told those two asses that I can produce witnesses to say that Athol was a changed man with something weighing on his mind. I want you to tell them that you thought he was different too. It is my considered opinion that he was being deliberately tormented as a prelude to being murdered."

The girl glanced away. "If you talked like this to Dr Spenser and Tom, I don't blame them for snubbing you."

Charles stared at her. "I received the impression earlier that you thought there was a possibility of Athol having been murdered."

She shrugged and did not answer.

"What has altered you? Is it because murder is something that might upset your well-ordered life? You're frightened of becoming involved in something for which you have no yardstick of behaviour?"

"You're not only absurd, but rude. There has been no murder."

"So careful—so discreet! Athol's murder is none of your business, so you just ignore it as an unpleasant interlude, or—" he stopped, searching for a way in which to shake her aggravating equanimity, "or are you falling into line because you're frightened of becoming too involved? By jove, I hadn't thought of that. I've been visualising the murderer as a vague figure who had stalked Athol to this district. I hadn't seriously considered that it might be someone from here in this—this contrived setting. I'm grateful to you for having pointed out the suspects."

But Shelagh was not to be goaded. "Would you mind going to your breakfast now? It holds us up if people are late for meals."

"I'm not having breakfast until I get this business fixed up," said Charles sulkily.

"You'll feel a lot better when you've eaten something," she said reasonably. "And goodness knows what Aunt Grace is saying in there."

IV

Wearing the shocked face which she kept for deaths, seductions and exorbitant butchers' bills, Miss Bryce had spread the news of Athol Sefton's death. She was now lecturing the guests on the proven foolhardiness of having anything to do with firearms and the care they must take in the next few days if the season was not to end up a liability to the Duck and Dog.

Adelaide Dougall sat watching her parents plough purposefully through their meal. If anything the news had served to stimulate their appetites, already sharpened by months of privation at their cheap boarding house. Not even they would have dreamed of the thoughts passing through their daughter's mind—unbidden thoughts that Adelaide was incapable of banishing now. They had come to her the previous evening and all through the night she had kept waking up with them, her heart pounding with fear, excitement and triumph. She had shown little shock at the news of Athol Sefton's death.

Mrs Dougall summoned Charles peremptorily, as she had been wont to summon her husband's junior officers. Her large, commanding figure was dressed in a suit the colour and texture of sacking, the skirt of which would retain a bulge for quite some time after she stood up. She had a parade-ground voice and about as much sensibility as a tank. "Well, young man!" she boomed, staring at Charles with pale protruding eyes. "What's this shocking business we hear about your uncle?"

Charles, annoyed with himself for obeying her summons and with the soundness of Shelagh's advice about having something to eat, was betrayed into rash utterance. "More shocking than you think. It is my opinion that Athol was not shot accidentally but murdered."

He turned his back on her, dragged out a chair from the adjoining table, and reached for the nearest thing to eat, which was toast from Wilson's rack. Shelagh brought him some coffee, putting the cup and saucer down with a near approach to a bang. He did not even thank her, but went on eating wolfishly, rejoicing in his sudden madness and the gratifying stunned silence about him. Even the mellowing influence of bacon and eggs did not bring about remorse, for the way the room cleared silently convinced him that he had not only shocked but frightened the other guests.

Beside him, Wilson slid out of his chair, then paused uncertainly, trying to speak. Charles looked at him challengingly. "Well, what is it?"

"D—did you f—?"

"For heavens' sake, what?"

"Fire your gun?"

"If you are asking—did I shoot Athol—no! He was killed by someone fifty yards or more away—using a rifle. A bullet killed him, not shot."

Wilson shook his head and started to mouth again.

"Oh, this is impossible," Charles muttered, glancing up as Ellis Bryce came sauntering into the room.

He was wearing sandals, ancient flannels and a bright yellow pullover over his pyjama jacket. "Shelagh, my dear, breakfast! Now don't reproach me about being late. You should know that I consider it quite beneath me to follow the herd and be on time for meals. Ah, good morning, Mr Wilson. Charles, I have greeted earlier. Judging from the expostulatory remarks passing my door, I gather you have announced poor Athol's untimely decease. I also gather by a certain moroseness in your demeanour that our good but mentally lacking friends, Spenser and Motherwell, did not appeal to you. Ah, thank you, Shelagh! Where is Jerry this morning? Grace, I can hear dropping saucepans."

"Still in bed, I suppose," said the girl off-handedly, uncovering the fried egg and sausage she had been keeping hot.

Ellis shook his head. "He wasn't five minutes ago, when I went to get this pullover." He had a habit of borrowing clothes he fancied. "Now if Athol were here—how I miss the bad fellow, already, Charles—he would immediately ask if I had looked in Margot's room. What was that, Mr Wilson?"

The little man blinked and mouthed, "I s-saw him g-g-"

"You saw him go out? Dear me, how unlike my son to be abroad before breakfast."

"Jerry often goes for a walk before breakfast," said Shelagh, clearing plates from the Dougalls' table.

Charles glanced at her, then at Ellis who met his eyes blandly. "Ah quite, my dear, I forgot. And his walk always takes him in the opposite direction from Teal Lagoon. Nota bene, Charles."

"Have you finished, Mr Wilson?" asked Shelagh, adding more plates to her tray.

He leapt aside, but remained nearby, hovering and uncertain. Suddenly he put a hand into a pocket and produced a card which he put on the table in front of Charles. "I'll h-have to con- con-"

Ellis picked up the card. "Confiscate your gun. Well, well! Not an anthropologist, after all. A field inspector from Fisheries and Game. I must tell Grace."

"Oh, so that's who you are. Athol thought he'd seen you before. Sorry to upset your ill-timed officialism, Mr Wilson, but my gun hasn't been used. You may inspect it if you wish."

"Mr Sefton's is the one you want," said Ellis helpfully, "though how that penalises Athol now, I can't see."

Charles said truculently, "I bet if Athol were here, he wouldn't allow anyone to lay a finger on it. You'll find both guns in the hall rack." He waited until Wilson had gone, then added, "I'm not sure that Greenet doesn't belong to me now."

Ellis, spreading marmalade thickly, raised his brows. "Is that so, indeed? Athol's beneficiary. Congratulations."

"Athol wouldn't have much to leave. But there should be my aunt's money."

Ellis licked his forefinger delicately. "What an invidious position that places you in—almost as bad as my tempestuous son's habit of not taking a walk before breakfast. Ah, the number of detective stories that feature that solitary pointless walk. I gather from Shelagh's praiseworthy attempt that, although she does not approve of your ideas how Athol met his death, she does not altogether discredit them."

"Your idea originally," conceded Charles, thinking he had an ally in Ellis. "I confess I thought it in poor taste at first."

"You mustn't let the notion obsess you. There is no one more tedious than a person with an *idée fixe*. To be quite frank, I find myself already losing interest in the subject. Before it wanes completely, tell me of the sufferings you endured from our worthy medico."

Charles paused in the act of lighting a cigarette to make an eloquent face.

"You found him pompous, oppressed with the dignity and power of his profession and entirely brainless?"

"Entirely. Motherwell likewise. Any suggestion on my part that further investigation into what they insisted could only be an accident was regarded as unwarranted. I shall take great pleasure in showing up their criminal stupidity."

"And how do you intend to do that?" asked Ellis, smothering a yawn as he helped himself to one of Charles's cigarettes.

"I need your co-operation."

Ellis looked startled. "My dear fellow, what can you mean?"

"I want your support in this business. It was your notion in the first place that Athol was murdered. You must help me."

"My dear chap, you don't want to take any notice of what I say before breakfast. What's more I take as much as a dozen notions a day. My latest is that Athol committed suicide. As for co-operating with anyone, I wouldn't know how. No really, Charles, I couldn't possibly mix on the same lowly plane as Motherwell."

Charles took a deep, exasperated breath. "Tell me, do you or do you not seriously consider Athol was murdered?"

Before Ellis could start saying that he never thought seriously about anything, certainly not immediately after breakfast, the door opened and Margot Stainsbury entered.

V

She was wearing black matador pants and a white shirt with pushed-up sleeves. There was a chunky gold bracelet on one slim arm and dangling rings in her small ears. Her eyes were round and innocent, her mouth a little open in a smile of studied childishness. She addressed Shelagh who had appeared at the kitchen door with a face so expressionless that Charles could only guess what she was thinking of the latecomer.

"So drefful sowwy! But such a ghastly night I had. I felt so haggish I simply had to have a little more sleepy-bye."

Charles remembered Margot's bouts of baby-talk of old. "Just some fruit and black coffee like an angel—oh, and a teeny piece of toast, very thin and crisp. Can do?"

She pirouetted on one flat shoe and said in the same breath, "And they say the country is quiet, Chas! All those frightful bird and animal noises—did they keep you awake too?" She flashed a smile at Ellis. "Aren't we city people just too dismal!"

"Devastatingly so," agreed Ellis. "I trust that is the right reply. This bucolic specimen is not up on the latest phraseology. Do please sit down opposite where I can gaze on your deliciously haggish countenance."

She sank into a chair and rested her chin on the back of one delicate hand. "I absolutely adore the things you say. Do you mind if I call you Ellis?"

"Not in the least, but Jerry might."

"Oh—Jerry!" she smiled tolerantly. "I'm furious with him. He behaved so badly last night. I told him I was going straight back to town today."

Ellis murmured to Charles, "Now I come to think of it, Shelagh was partly right. I seem to recall Jerry tramping the countryside last year too."

"Of course Athol can be an absolute swine," stated Margot. "I could have simply murdered him myself. In fact—what are you making such faces for, Chas? Are you ill, darling?"

Ellis scraped back his chair, took another of Charles's cigarettes and yawned. "You must forgive me if I leave now. I cannot abide re-iteration. Furthermore, I offered in a misguided moment last night to give the herd some target practice in preparation for tomorrow's blaze away."

Shelagh came in with Margot's breakfast. "Jerry's having his in the kitchen," she informed the room at large. "And he did go in the opposite direction from Teal Lagoon."

"So yah! The pair of us!" said Ellis from the doorway as he slopped out.

"What in the world is the matter with them?" asked Margot. "Jerry can have breakfast in the fowl yard for all I care. Such a trying boy, Chas. What makes me take up with neurotics? Oh sorry, darling—present company excepted of course. Anyway you were never really in love with me." She put out a hand to pat his.

Charles caught hold of it. "Margot, something terrible has happened. Athol is dead."

Her scarlet nails pressed slowly into his skin. "Charles!" she put up her free hand to her cheek in a shocked gesture. "Oh, poor Athol! How—why—"

"I don't know exactly yet, but he didn't die naturally."

Her large eyes were fixed on his face. "What do you mean?"

"He was shot. We went out early this morning after duck, to that place they call Teal Lagoon. It is my theory that someone followed us there and took up a position waiting to kill Athol."

Margot gave a horrified gasp. "Charles, do you know what you're saying!"

"Yes, I know. Now don't get into a flap like a good girl. I know you were fond of Athol, but you're as tough as they come actually."

"But Chas, this is absurd, frightful, I don't know which. You should have broken it more gently. You always were a clumsy-tongued creature." She put both her hands over her face for a moment, but not too roughly so as to disturb her skilful make-up, then emerged looking dewy-eyed. "Charles, they don't really think Athol was murdered, do they?"

He deplored the loose pronoun. "If by 'they' you mean the local authorities—no, they don't. They think Athol was killed accidentally by another duck-shooter. For several reasons to which they refused to listen, I think Athol was murdered. You know one of those reasons yourself, Margot."

She looked startled. "No, I don't. Now Charles, don't be silly. I told you before you made too much of a thing of this detective business. Don't you remember?"

"Yes, I remember. I can also recall the occasion when you issued that rebuke. At a cocktail party when you were talking to me about Athol's odd behaviour in Sydney, and how you thought he was haunted."

"Did I say that?" she asked lightly, after an almost imperceptible pause. "I can't recall exactly, but if you say so, darling, I won't deny it."

"You'd better not deny it," he said good-humouredly, hoping to coax away the slightly guarded look that had come over her face. "I want you to tell Sergeant Motherwell that you had also noticed a change in Athol and about that mysterious phone call he received while lunching with you at Manonetta's. You wouldn't want the person who killed Athol to get away with it, would you? Imagine, Margot—someone was deliberately playing on his nerves before finally murdering him!"

She lit a cigarette, inserting it in her long, tortoise-shell holder with fingers that trembled slightly. "Damn, I'm as nervy as a cat. I feel ghastly over this, Chas. I simply can't believe that Athol was actually murdered. What I mean is—who would have done such a thing?"

"Someone staying here at the Duck and Dog."

She stared at him for a moment, then her lids lowered and a little smile played around her mouth. He knew that expression of old. You could go so far with Margot, but when she chose to stop there was no forcing her on. "Oh now, Chas!" she said in an amused voice. "You can't really mean what you say. It just doesn't make sense. I know quite a few people hated poor Athol, but no one would actually murder him. Darling, you're trying to complicate something which is quite simple. You know, dear," she went on, changing to earnestness, "I don't think you've looked a bit well lately. All that writing about detective novels—you've got murder on your mind."

Next she'll be telling me I need a holiday, thought Charles.

She got up and came round to put an affectionate arm around his shoulders. "Believe me, Charles, I know just how you feel. Just as soon as this dreadful business is wound up, you must get away from everything—take a trip somewhere."

"I've taken a trip," said Charles. "I came here—and here I am going to stay until I find out who killed Athol."

"Darling, do be reasonable! You can't go round poking and prying. Goodness knows what you'll turn up."

"Which is precisely what I hope will happen. Someone here hated Athol with more than the usual animosity he aroused—enough to murder him."

"You are going to make yourself terribly disliked," she said on a sigh.

"I can bear it. Why the sudden anxiety for my feelings?"

"Because I'm fond of you, Chas. I always have been. It hurts me to see you making a fool of yourself."

"It doesn't hurt you another way, does it? I find the reluctance of people to believe me somewhat strange."

"Well, darling, you can't expect them to. Frankly, I don't. I think you're just crazy. And I am very sorry, Charles, but I utterly refuse to be any party to this mad idea of yours."

"In other words you don't intend to tell Motherwell about that phone call at Manonetta's. All right, then," Charles shook off her arm and got up.

"What are you going to do?"

"I've told you—find out who killed Athol. And I warn you, Margot, that your refusal to help me means that you automatically join the list of suspects."

"I adored Athol," she declared indignantly.

He gazed at her speculatively with half-closed eyes, as though seeing her in another way. "No, you didn't—not always anyway. Last night you loathed him. You said only a while back that you could have murdered him. It could have been you who was tormenting him with threatening messages and phone calls. Perhaps you made a point of telling me about his strange change merely to cover yourself. You knew he was going out early this morning. You could have got out of the house unseen and followed us, then—"

"Margot did not shoot Sefton," said a vibrant voice behind them. They swung round. Jerry Bryce stood at the kitchen doorway. "She knows nothing. I killed him."

For a long moment they stared at him while he glared back with dark burning eyes. He was an incredibly handsome young man with highly combustible moods and a complete lack of humour. It was a small wonder that Athol had found him such easy bait.

"Margot did not shoot Sefton," he said again. He knew the value of repetition, for although he called himself a playwright, his main livelihood was derived from writing radio serials of the soap-opera variety.

Charles, torn between exasperation and amusement, let out a moan. "Oh no, I will not have someone confessing to the crime. It's against all the rules."

"Of course I didn't shoot Athol," Margot snapped. "I've never fired a gun in my life."

"That's what you say," said Charles provokingly.

Jerry came forward, head up and fists clenched. "Are you calling Miss Stainsbury a liar?"

"Not on this occasion—yet. But I've known her to tell the biggest whoppers ever when it suited her."

"Oh, Chas! Now Jerry dear, don't get intense. It's frightfully sweet of you to be chivalrous, but honestly there's no need—is there, Charles?"

"Well, I'm not so sure," said Charles musingly.

"Absolutely no need," repeated Margot, shooting him a kindling glance, "because, of course, poor Athol was not murdered. The police say he was shot accidentally."

"Stop calling him poor Athol," said Charles peevishly, who was feeling a championship for him in death that he had never had in life.

Jerry looked from one to the other, nonplussed. "Well, actually I didn't kill him," he admitted, "though I could have done so. I went out for a walk and no one saw me and I loathed Sefton's guts. What's more, although I'm not a frightfully good shot, Father has a couple of rifles in the gunroom."

"I'll put you right at the top of the suspect list," said Charles in admiration. "Your confession was a fake—a put-up arrangement between you and Margot—but I shan't allow it to put me off the scent."

"Charles, will you stop acting the fool over this ghastly affair?"

"I'm perfectly serious. Jerry is the first one I've found ready to face up to reality. The reluctance of everyone else to do the same encourages my belief that Athol was deliberately murdered."

"If you say once more that Athol was murdered," said Margot in high tones, "I'll scream." As a sudden volley of gun-shot sounded close at hand at this juncture, she unwittingly carried out her threat.

VI

Ellis had once had the brilliant notion of constructing a shooting range for the amusement and improvement of the Duck and Dog guests. That was five years ago and the targets of the practice ground, which was a paddock just the other side of the rickety corrugated iron construction called the garages, had not advanced beyond a few cans scattered around and a couple of fortuitous tree stumps on which to place them.

Major and Mrs Dougall were blazing away at these with all the prodigal enthusiasm of gunsmen supplied with free ammunition. Mrs Dougall had a cartridge belt strapped athwart her mighty bosom and the Major was wearing a tweed hat to match his suit, which was already decorated with bedraggled-looking feathers as camouflage for the following day. Ellis, propped lazily against the wall of the shed, was keeping up a satiric conversation with the American, who was examining the group of shotguns brought out from the gunroom for practice firing.

"In this country we don't go in for all the elaborate specialisation that you people seem to devote to the sport. When I'm feeling equal to the strain of listening—you may remind me this evening in the bar—you must give the assembly an account of your various organisations."

"I didn't know we had any," said Jeffrey, squinting down the barrel of a rusty Purdie and flicking the bolt. "Too bad you've let these guns go—if you don't mind my saying so."

"I don't mind in the least," replied Ellis amiably. "I have frequently deplored their state myself. Unfortunately my sister Grace flatly refuses to handle firearms, unloaded or not. Perhaps if I were to deplore more vehemently in my son's hearing? Here he comes now with the incomparable Margot and the bereaved Charles." He waited for them to come near. "Mr Jeffrey says the guns should be kept clean and oiled. He may not have heard of Ducks Unlimited, but he does know guns."

His eyes moved from Jerry's scowling face to Charles's quick look of interest, then to Margot who appeared a little dazed. "Ah! I see you have been told about Athol. Don't think we are not showing respect for the dead, my dear. As people always say when they wish to suit themselves—I am sure poor Athol would have wanted us to carry on just as usual. Pukka and Memsahib, as you can see and hear, are illustrating the point."

"That's my sweater you've got on," announced Jerry truculently.

"It is. I'm so relieved you won't want to wear it this morning as I find myself quite attached to it. Fair Margot, you must permit me to give you your first lesson in how to handle a gun." He calmly took the one Jeffrey was handling and loaded it from an open cartridge box nearby. Jerry followed them with an aggressive tread.

Left alone, the American said to Charles, "He sure is a funny guy. I've never met that type of wise-cracking before." There was a grin on his face, but Charles thought he detected an uneasiness about him.

"He is certainly inimitable. Have you been in this country long, Mr Jeffrey?"

"Four, five weeks."

"Business, or with the idea of settling?"

"Business. I made some contacts here during the war."

"What type of business would that be?"

The American squatted down and began to inspect another gun. One of the dogs rose, stretched itself and ambled up to nose at his hands. "Oh—just agencies for this and that."

"Was my uncle one of your contacts?"

"You mean the guy who was killed this morning? No, I never met him before last evening." He looked up as he spoke, one hand holding the gun across his knees, the other fingering the dog's ears.

"This is a rather out-of-the-way place for you to be, isn't it?" asked Charles.

"It was recommended as a good place for hunting wild-fowl. Perhaps you'd like to come and watch me tomorrow morning?"

"No, thanks, I've had a stomach full of duck-shooting already."

The American got to his feet leisurely. "Any more questions?" he drawled.

Charles met his gaze. "Not at the moment."

"Then I guess I'll go and start getting my eye in." He picked up a gun and went across the paddock to where Margot was being prettily clumsy and Ellis was deriving more delight from annoying Jerry than in showing her how to handle a gun.

Charles watched the play, wondering if Margot was merely acting the part of novice. But when her first round went dangerously close to Major Dougall, causing him to turn into a pop-eyed lobster with indignation and fright, he was inclined to consider her manoeuvres genuine.

"Mr Carmichael!" said a soft deep voice. He turned and found Frances Turner gazing up at him earnestly. She was wearing neat jodhpurs and an open-necked shirt, and carried two shotguns under her arm, their barrels pointing to the ground. "Did you really mean what you said this morning? About Mr Sefton having been murdered?"

"Yes, I meant it," returned Charles. "Have you come to support the general attitude that I am making capital out of a situation that is my hobby?"

"Oh, no," she protested. "I know who you are, of course. My sister was a subscriber to *Culture and Critic* for years, and I always read your reviews though I don't care for detective novels for reading. I just wanted to say how sorry I—that is, Andy and I both are. It must be frightful having a relation whom you think was murdered."

He was amused by the naive way in which she expressed herself, and more than a little flattered by the admiring awe in which she apparently held him. "Then you don't think it so extraordinary that my uncle was murdered?"

"Well, it's not for me to give an opinion," she replied hesitantly. "Especially as the police, so I understand, consider it was an accident, but—"

"But?" Charles prompted, touched by her simplicity after the complexity of the others he had spoken to.

She looked at the ground. "I hope you don't think I'm rude, but—but he wasn't a very nice person, was he? I mean—well, neither Andy nor I cared much for him even at first meeting last night."

"He didn't impress you then, as a person who would improve upon acquaintance? You're right—he wasn't. But people don't go around murdering unlikeable men as a general rule. What I have to find is someone who hated Athol enough to torment him before finally killing him. Such hate is, I should say, rather rare."

Frances stared at him uncomprehendingly. He smiled. "I was only thinking aloud. I'm sorry Athol embarrassed you last night. He only did it to tease."

She nodded. "That's what I told Andy. I'm afraid he was furious though." She paused, as though to pluck up courage to ask an important question. "Are you going to find out who did it, Mr Carmichael?"

"I hope to," he replied guardedly. "But I'm not progressing very rapidly. You see, I have to prove murder first, and the persons I counted on to help have backed out."

"What a shame!" she declared warmly.

Again he was amused. "Well, you can't blame them entirely. They're scared of being suspected of the crime."

Her eyes widened. "I hadn't thought of that. You mean that someone—one of us here—?"

"Precisely, Mrs Turner. I believe that someone came here with the primary purpose of shooting, not ducks, but Athol."

She looked frightened and cast a glance over her shoulder at the group near the targets. Andrew had joined them and was striding about talking loudly on their shooting merits. He shouted across to his wife. "Hurry up there, Frankie!"

"I must go," she said, but paused in flight. "Andy wasn't really furious, Mr Carmichael. He thought it a bit of a joke actually—the way Mr Sefton spoke to us."

Charles gazed after her thoughtfully, and saw her speaking rapidly to her husband as she handed him one of the guns. Andrew shot a belligerent glance in his direction and made a threatening step forward, but he was restrained by Frances's hand on his arm. Then he threw back his head and laughed, and said something to the others.

Good! thought Charles recklessly. The sooner everybody knows I'm serious about Athol's murder, the better.

Mrs Dougall's booming tones reached him. "I never heard anything like it in my life. Jumbo! You'll have to speak to that impertinent young man."

Splendid, thought Charles. Come on, Jumbo, I'm ready. Ah, coward! For Major Dougall had cravenly appealed to Ellis, who, with a tact wholly unlike him, evidently uttered some soothing words and set the target practice in motion again. Presently he left the group and came over to Charles.

"My dear fellow, I wish you'd go away. You're demoralising my guests."

"Good!"

"Not good at all. A joke's a joke, so they tell me, though in my experience most jokes are fiendishly unfunny—as witness the Dougalls' rising choler on this occasion. You will have the pukka sahib dying of apoplexy and really, on top of Athol's sad demise, the Duck and Dog will be getting what Grace is always fearing—a bad name. Do go away and play your games elsewhere."

"I'm pleased to see I've got even you rattled, Ellis."

"Quite unnerved, I assure you. Whether Athol was shot accidentally or on purpose I don't care, but I foresee my peace being absolutely destroyed by people wanting me to do something about you. For my sake, at least be a bit more tactful."

"I'll go away presently. I want to see who can shoot and who can't. Margot is the only one out so far."

"Didn't she make a wonderful muddle! But with your lynx eyes observing, what did you expect?"

"You mean she was pretending? She said she'd never fired a gun in her life."

"I often find, my dear Charles, that when a woman uses the phrase 'never in my life' there are usually some fairly consistent exceptions. But to be just to the enchanting girl, at least she did not come here pretending to shoot ducks."

"One of the names you are not naming being Harris P. Jeffrey? I take it that he should have heard of Ducks Unlimited if he were genuine. Thanks for the tip. I only wish you would co-operate altogether."

"I couldn't stand up to the strain," said Ellis plaintively. "You may avail yourself of any gems of wisdom that should fall from my lips, of course, but I can't promise to be always in a communicative mood. Do watch the nice piece of shooting Mrs Turner is putting on. Husband-coached, I should say from the ultra-possessive expression on the spouse's face. It follows that Andrew must be what is known as a crack shot."

Charles turned to watch and when he looked round again Ellis had gone. Instead Adelaide Dougall stood alongside. "Hullo!" he said awkwardly, wondering how she was taking Athol's death. Her blushes and adoring glances in Athol's direction in the earlier part of the previous evening had been painfully obvious. Only Athol had remained unembarrassed, treating her so contumeliously that she could not have been left in any doubt as to his feelings for what he had termed ageing nymphomaniacs.

She just stood there staring at him steadily, a look that made him blink nervously. "So you think he was murdered!" she said at last.

"You mean Athol?" Charles queried foolishly.

She nodded impatiently, still watching him with that disconcerting stare.

"Er—yes, I think there is the possibility. You see—" he broke off. Then for some inexplicable reason he added lamely, "Actually the police say it was an accident and perhaps they are right, but—"

She leaned towards him. "But you are convinced he was murdered, aren't you?" Her eyes were gleaming now with a strange excitement. "And you suspect one of us of having done it. I think he was murdered too. In fact, I know it. But there is just one matter I want to bring to your attention, Mr Carmichael." She came nearer and Charles backed away, his chin in his neck. "You'll never find out who did it. What do you say to that?"

"Er—nothing much. I mean—probably I won't. Look will you excuse me? I—ah—have to go now."

He escaped round the garages, pausing there to wipe his forehead. The poor girl's gone dotty, he thought. The only one to agree with my conviction. A nice fool I'd look if I got her to substantiate my theories to the police.

There were voices in Athol's room as Charles passed on the way to his own. He opened the door and Shelagh and Miss Bryce turned round.

"Ah—here he is now!" said the latter. "The very person—you needn't fold the blankets, Shelagh. I want to air them."

"What are you doing here?" demanded Charles. The room had been stripped of Athol's belongings which the girl was packing with an amazing economy of space and neatness into his pig-skin bags. "Who told you to touch my uncle's things?"

"No one," replied Shelagh calmly, placing a pile of beautifully folded shirts in last and closing one bag with a snap. "Is there any reason why we should not?"

"Every reason and you know it," Charles flung at her, striding over to the dressing table and opening drawers.

"Everything from there is in the other bag," Miss Bryce informed him. "What do you want done with Mr Sefton's things?"

"I wanted them left where they were for the time being. Goodness knows what might be mislaid now. Where is his briefcase?"

"Behind you on the table," said Shelagh, picking up a pile of review books and inspecting the titles. Charles snatched it up and undid the zipper so hastily that papers fell to the floor.

"Now, isn't that just like a man!" declared Miss Bryce crossly, bending down to sweep them together. "Why are you acting so hasty, young man? We haven't taken anything belonging to your precious uncle."

"I just didn't want anything touched until I had—ah, you've missed something," he broke off to say in an accusing voice. From floor level he had noticed a pair of shoes half under the bed.

Shelagh glanced up. "I knew they were there. I intended taking them to clean before packing."

"That's what—" Charles began rudely. "Clean? Why should they need cleaning?" He stood upright, the shoes in one hand.

"Well, isn't it obvious?" asked Miss Bryce tartly, as a piece of dried mud fell onto the carpet and sent her bending again.

Charles felt a sudden glow. "Because," he said triumphantly, "they shouldn't need cleaning. When and where would Athol have worn them to get them in such a state?"

Shelagh went on glancing through the books with an elaborate disinterest, but Miss Bryce, who could never let even a piece of rhetoric go by, said, "How should we know? It's nothing to do with us what—please be careful! You're still dropping bits of mud. Perhaps they're not Mr Sefton's shoes."

Charles turned them over. "They're Athol's all right. I know the Sydney store where he shops. I also know the rubber tread on the soles—now. Would you like me to tell you how the shoes got so dirty?"

Shelagh said, "Not particularly," but Miss Bryce, feeling something was expected of her, said vaguely, "If you want to—though I'm sure I don't know why you are making such a song and dance about a pair of shoes."

"Mr Carmichael thinks his uncle was murdered, Aunt Grace, and that one of us did it."

Miss Bryce looked from her niece to Charles between doubt and dismay. "I don't really think so—I'm convinced," said Charles. "Now about these shoes. This morning I found prints in the soft ground near the lagoon about a hundred yards from where Athol stood up in the boat. The person who shot him realised that the leaving of footprints would be unavoidable and in order to disguise his own wore Athol's shoes."

He paused expectantly, but this Miss Bryce only remarked dampingly, "Just fancy that! Shelagh, I'll take these blankets down to the line." She bundled them together and went out.

A stifled sound made Charles glance at the girl. Her eyes were twinkling and she was biting her lips. "Oh, very funny!" he said sourly.

"Perhaps you'll realise now how ridiculous your notions are."

"Ridiculous!" he almost shouted. "You don't think I'm doing all this just for the fun of it, do you? Someone from here shot Athol—had all the intentions of killing him for some time. A cooler, cleverer and more deliberately planned murder you wouldn't find in the best detective fiction today—and because I recognise it as such you call me ridiculous!"

"Well, you needn't shout, just because no one else agrees with you."

"No one agrees with me for the simple reason that they are scared."

"I'm not in the least bit scared," she said coldly.

"Yes, you are. You think Jerry might have shot Athol—that stood out a mile this morning."

"Of course Jerry didn't shoot Athol."

"He could have. He said he did."

"What!"

Charles grinned suddenly. "He thought I was accusing Margot, so he came to her rescue with a confession. Made quite a good fist of it too—explaining how your father keeps a couple of rifles in the gunroom. By jove—" he stopped, his forehead wrinkling.

"What is it?" asked Shelagh sharply.

"I'm wondering if one of your father's rifles was used. After all, if the murderer borrowed a pair of shoes, it would be nothing to borrow the weapon. I've got a hunch that that was the case."

"I thought you didn't hold with hunches," she said maliciously.

"In books, no," he returned cheerfully. "But this is real life."

"I don't know if it is real," said Shelagh slowly. "You've made everything seem so crazy and—and frightening."

He turned back from the door to say soothingly, "You keep on packing while I look for your father. Sling the things into my room when you've finished. And if you come across anything that looks like a clue, please don't suppress it. I rate rock bottom those books where some female invariably gums up the case."

Ellis was seated in the bar with his feet on another chair, alternately sipping contentedly at a long cold drink and carrying on a one-sided conversation with Wilson, who was drawing judicious draughts of lemonade through a straw. The latter had evidently been trying to impress upon Ellis the need to keep his identity as a field inspector a secret until after the following day's blaze-away.

Ellis was taking delight in misunderstanding the other's earnest inarticulation, but when Charles burst in he said with an amiable wave of his hand, "All right—all right! Mum's the word, as I read somewhere in the literature of my youth. Charles, you mustn't tell the pukka sahib who Wilson is. He wants to catch him being naughty."

"How many rifles have you precisely?"

Ellis groaned. "Don't tell me you're still at it! I would rather play Mr Wilson's games for a while."

Charles knocked Ellis's feet off the chair and sat down. "Now, listen to me. I'm tired of your being obstructionist. If, for no other reason but to make Spenser and Motherwell look the pair of fools they are, you've got to co-operate. I've found a significant piece of evidence which, if I can tie it up with the murder weapon, will prove that Athol wasn't killed accidentally."

Ellis scraped his chair forward and put his feet on the table instead. "He wears me out, this young man does, Mr Wilson. What do you suggest that I do?"

Wilson said surprisingly, "Turner has a r—r—"

"Rifle? Has he, by jove!" exclaimed Charles. "Thanks for the tip. How do you know?"

"Snooping," said Ellis airily. "Mr Wilson's job, you know."

The field inspector reddened and essayed a painful explanation. It appears that he had been standing near the utility as Mrs Turner was unpacking the shotguns for practice firing. In telling him of her husband's prowess with kangaroos up north, she had shown him the Wilding.

"Ah, one of the prolific kind. Wildings, my poor Charles, abound in this country. They started manufacturing them late in the war, which fortunately ended before the paucity of their powers could be put to the test. I believe they are still cluttering up the disposals stores, though I did my bit by purchasing a couple. You'll find them in the gunroom—that is, if someone hasn't borrowed them."

"I'd be surprised if one at least hasn't been," said Charles grimly. "You'd better come with me and look."

Ellis gave another groan. "Mr Wilson, do you know the appearance of a Wilding? Go with this harassing young man."

"The time is rapidly approaching when you will just have to shake off your innate laziness," Charles told him roundly and followed the field inspector out of the room.

Going along the passage, Wilson said, "And J—J—Jeffrey has a re—v—volver."

"Athol wasn't shot with a revolver," said Charles absently. "I'm not interested. This is the room, isn't it?"

Wilson went round the racks pulling out guns, some of them so deteriorated that he was unable to break the breach. Presently he indicated one of the Wildings. "It looks as though it hasn't been fired for years," said Charles, inspecting it. "The lock's gone too, so that's out. Have another look for the other one. Both Ellis and Jerry said there were two."

Wilson did the rounds again and finally shook his head.

"Hah!" exclaimed Charles, in high good-humour. "Net result—one only Wilding. Thank you, Mr Wilson, for your services."

He strode back to the bar. "There's only one," he said, bursting into the room which was now full of people. Target practice was over and the guests had gathered for pre-luncheon drinks. They turned at Charles's tempestuous entrance.

"I must have lent it to someone," said Ellis comfortably. "Come and have your beer, boy, and stop wearing yourself out."

"To whom did you lend it?"

Ellis picked up his glass. "Can't remember rightly, but it stands to reason I must have."

"It doesn't stand to reason at all. I don't think you did lend it."

"What on earth are you two talking about?" asked Margot, who was perched on a stool with the easy grace of one accustomed to bar stools. She took a sip from the cocktail Jerry had just mixed for her and wrinkled her nose prettily. "Darling, far, far too much gin. But never mind, I'll drink it." She swallowed half and smiled bravely at Jerry's sulky face.

"Someone must have taken it," Charles was insisting in a low voice. "Surely you would remember if you had lent it."

"Chas, what's all the mutter-mutter? Speak up, dear, when you're in company." Margot chided, fitting a cigarette into her long holder and turning her big eyes onto the American, who sprang to light it.

"All right," said Ellis in a peaceable tone. "Someone took it—if it makes you happy. Who took a Wilding rifle out of the gunroom? Charles thinks someone borrowed it to shoot Athol Sefton. Is that right, Charles?"

"Yes, it is," he agreed furiously. "Damn you, Ellis, will you stop making a farce out of this affair?"

"My dear chap, better poor comedy than poor drama."

"Young man!" boomed Mrs Dougall, who was nursing a large sherry in place of the cartridge belt. "Are you accusing one of us of murdering your uncle with Ellis's Wilding?"

"I don't think it actually matters if it was not my particular gun," said Ellis, with the air of one making a concession.

"I've got a Wilding," said Andrew Turner, jutting his jaw at Charles. "I daresay you would like to have a look at it. It's all right, Frankie," he added, throwing off his wife's hand. "You leave this to me."

"But Andy, we hadn't even unpacked it. Mr Carmichael does not mean—"

"I don't care what he doesn't mean or does mean, but I think it's pretty hot that you can't choose to stay in a pub for a couple of days without being accused of the murder of a perfect stranger."

"I'm sorry, Mr Turner, but—" began Charles quietly.

"You can go on apologising to the rest of us," interrupted Mrs Dougall haughtily.

"I'm damned if I will!" said Charles, roused by her overbearing manner. "Someone here shot Athol deliberately and I apologise to no one for my suspicions until such time they can prove to me that they did not kill him."

"I thought you Aussies followed the British tradition that a man is innocent until proven guilty," drawled Jeffrey.

"You don't like Australians, do you? I wonder why you came here since you think so poorly of us."

"Don't you like us, really?" Margot asked, round-eyed and open-mouthed with provocative innocence.

The American's face relaxed into a grin. "Honey, I'd like you if you were an Eskimo. What do you say, folks, if we just pay no heed to this guy and his crazy ideas?"

"I'm in full agreement with you," declared Major Dougall, who had been hanging about nervously, waiting for a loophole such as this. "It's obvious the fellow can't behave like a gentleman."

Mrs Dougall did not care for convenient loopholes. "I still maintain something should be done about this impertinent young man. Ellis, you must put your foot down. After all you are more or less in authority here."

Ellis looked pained. "My dear lady, I never put my foot down at any time. I wouldn't know how to. I'm completely ruled by my family."

"You mean you won't! If I didn't know you so well, I might suggest you were afraid of this young man."

"How can I have possibly deceived you?" wondered Ellis. "For that is precisely what I am."

"Nonsense!" she gave Charles a disparaging appraisal. "I can't see much to be afraid of."

"It's fear of exertion that is Father's worry," declared Jerry, with unfilial contempt. "He doesn't care what happens as long as you all make fools of yourselves and keep him amused. And that includes you, Charles."

"I don't understand what you are talking about," stated Mrs Dougall flatly. "Jumbo! Will you kindly make a stand in this matter?"

The Major gulped down the rest of his whisky and soda, touched his wiry moustache and squared his shoulders with a harrumph.

"Gad, sir!" muttered Jerry derisively, and turned to glare balefully at Jeffrey who was alleviating Margot's boredom with the discussion.

"Mr Carmichael," began the Major, forcefully enough. "We all realise that your uncle's death has been a great shock—"

"Just a minute," interrupted Charles. "You knew Athol fairly well, did you not?"

"I have been acquainted with him over a period of years. But that is beside the point. The assembled gathering here—"

"I understand the acquaintanceship extended beyond a mutual antipathy at the Duck and Dog?"

"I had a certain business acquaintance with him," admitted the Major stiffly. "Though how that affects the present issue I fail to understand."

"I often think people who use the phrase 'I fail to understand', understand only too well," put in Ellis musingly from the corner, where he had retired to watch proceedings.

"I agree with you," said Charles. "I understand quite well, Major Dougall, that you once went to Athol for advice on investing money, and that his advice was unfortunately not as sound as it should have been."

The Major's colour rose with his voice. "I resent this inquisition, sir. What have my financial matters to do with you?"

"No doubt you bore my uncle a certain grudge over the failure of his advice?" persisted Charles.

"I repeat, sir," the other shouted, "that is none of your business. You are an undisciplined young cub, and your uncle was nothing short of a rogue."

"Jumbo!" said Mrs Dougall sharply.

"I'm afraid I can't apologise to you yet, Major," said Charles smoothly, and made an ironic bow towards Mrs Dougall.

"I think that perhaps Mr Jeffrey has the right idea," announced Mrs Dougall, giving the American the slight gracious bow she used to keep for young up-and-coming officers. "We will all of us disregard this—er—exceedingly difficult young man. "

VII

After lunch Charles took his car from the garage and drove into Dunbavin. He had no difficulty in locating the police station, but quite a deal in raising Sergeant Motherwell who, with his report on Athol Sefton's death all written up ready for the inquest the following day, was enjoying a well-earned siesta. He lay stretched out on the leather-covered bench in his office under the ferocious hirsute gazes of by-gone custodians of law and order in Dunbavin.

His dreams were slightly troubled by a subconscious thought of the cocky young chap who seemed bent on disrupting the smooth procedure of his official duties. Perhaps this was because of the telephone call from the Duck and Dog which had interrupted his meal just as his mother had placed before him a large serving of suet roll oozing jam. He dreamed that young Carmichael was attacking him with his own baton and raining down blows on his head. Although he felt no pain, he could hear the sounds of the blows and they sounded so much like wood upon wood that he awakened indignantly, at first blaming the pudding and then becoming conscious of someone knocking at the front door.

Hurriedly, he pulled on his boots, gave a tug to his tunic and went to answer the summons. "Oh, it's you!" he said, not in the least surprised to see Charles. The aura of his dream was still with him and he eyed Charles carefully. A baton was no crazier than the pair of muddy laced brogues that the young fellow carried in one hand.

"Evidence," announced Charles, lifting them up. "And I think I've found the murder weapon—at least, not found it precisely but one of Ellis Bryce's Wildings is missing."

Sergeant Motherwell shook his head, trying to clear away that heaviness. "Now then, what's all this about?" he demanded.

Unwillingly he led the way to the office and seated himself at the desk on which lay his report, neatly but laboriously typed that morning. He gave a palpable wince when Charles placed Athol's shoes on top of it, moving them ostentatiously to one side and regarding them with no less distaste when he heard the explanation of their presence.

He listened phlegmatically to Charles's theories, then pointed out that the sole design could be a common one. As for the footprint he had found near Teal Lagoon, it could undoubtedly belong to the person who shot Sefton—accidentally.

"Then, even if it was not someone from the Duck and Dog who wore these shoes, are you going to do nothing about finding your so-called careless shooter?" asked Charles angrily.

"That will be for the Coroner to decide," was the reply. As to the missing Wilding—had not Bryce stated that he must have lent it to someone?

"Who told you that?"

"A gentleman called Dougall rang to complain about you," said the sergeant severely. "He said you were making everyone's life a misery out at Bryce's. Now see here, Mr Carmichael, if you can't behave like a reasonable man and stop making a nuisance of yourself, I'll have to find some way in which to make you."

Charles closed his lips on an angry retort. He realised he had aroused too much prejudice already and that his best course now was to play down his convictions, at least until the inquest. After enquiring more quietly when this would be, he took himself off.

Sergeant Motherwell saw him go with relief, and after congratulating himself on his diplomatic handling of a hot-headed young crank, went back to his interrupted slumber.

Dr Spenser was another Dunbavinite who believed in an after-luncheon nap on Sundays. His slumber was guarded by that excellent help-mate, Mrs Spenser, who early in marriage had constituted herself as a sort of bull-dog between the noble profession of her husband and that heedless, inconsiderate conglomerate of persons known as patients.

She did not, however, take into account a visitor such as Charles. Seeing a sign above the side door marked 'Surgery', he stalked straight in without ringing or knocking, thus surprising the doctor with his shoes off and his open mouth showing the slipped upper plate of his dentures.

Charles awakened him by rapping on the desk. He sat up hurriedly, just managing to shut his mouth before the upper plate fell out.

"Hullo, young fellow!" he said irritably. "What do you think you're doing here?"

"Sorry if I disturbed you. I wanted to know what you've done with Athol."

"I had the undertaker over. Do you want to make arrangements about a funeral?"

"Yes, I suppose I'd better do something about that. Tell me, did you succeed in getting the bullet out?"

"Naturally," said the doctor testily, feeling about for his shoes.

"Where is it? Do you mind if I have a look?"

"No, I don't mind, I suppose. But I can't remember where I put it precisely."

"What!" ejaculated Charles. "You don't remember where you put an important piece of evidence like the bullet!"

The doctor put on his rimless spectacles in order to increase the haughtiness of his stare. "I don't like your tone, young man. The bullet is superfluous. All that is necessary is contained in my report."

"I must find it," said Charles fretfully, slapping his hand over the desk in case it was under papers. "For heaven's sake will you try to remember what you did with it?"

"Kindly stop touching my belongings and get out of here. I didn't ask you in to start with, and to finish I don't like you—or your uncle."

"Which is why you've hidden the bullet," accused Charles wildly.

"Hidden? Why should I—now, look here, young man, have you gone mad?"

"I'm the one sane person in this whole crazy affair," retorted Charles. "The only one with enough honesty and common sense to realise that Athol was murdered, not shot by accident."

"Are you still clinging to that ludicrous notion? I advise you to watch your step."

"I'm watching it—and others' as well. Did you put it down somewhere carefully or throw it out?"

The doctor said coldly, "If you mean the bullet, it's probably in the swab bucket in the other room. If you just stay quietly for a moment I'll take a look." With a last wary glance, he went out. After a few minutes he came back. "Here you are!"

"I note that you found it pretty quickly when you saw I was in earnest. Tell me, what sort of gun would you say this fitted?"

The doctor's face quivered with dislike, but he replied equably, "Probably a Wilding—like that one of mine in the corner."

Charles swung round. "You own a Wilding?"

"Certainly. Why do you ask?"

"The inference is obvious, I'd say," retorted Charles and took his leave.

VIII

The duck season opened officially at five a.m. on Monday, March the second. All over the State of Victoria, sportsmen (and women) waited at swamps, lakes and rivers for the chilly dawn to break.

Quite a few opened up before the set time, thus spoiling the fun for others. But at Teal Lagoon near the Duck and Dog, the party was kept strictly to schedule under the frosty eye of Major Dougall. He had set his watch by Eastern Standard Time the previous night and checked off the minutes in a voice of mounting tension as though planning a surprise assault on the Khyber Pass. As Margot stated to Charles later—the pukka sahib made it sound exciting even though it was the most boring affair she had ever been at.

In the glorious blaze-away which followed, the unpleasant affairs of the day before were forgotten. The only contretemps which marred proceedings was the claiming of a bird which both Jerry Bryce and the American insisted they had brought down. This developed into a three-sided contest when Wilson announced that the bird was a shoveller and they should not have shot it anyway. The disclosure of the field inspector's identity reduced Charles's position on the scale of unpopularity, and they were still arguing hotly as to who should pay the fine when they returned to the hotel for breakfast.

Nothing was said about attending the inquest on Athol Sefton, but there was a general casual leaning towards the idea of taking a jaunt into the town. When Charles set off later in the morning he smiled grimly at the reflection of a string of cars in his rear-vision mirror.

The Mechanics Institute was crowded with people who had heard curious rumours concerning the Sunday accident. There were whispers and pointings as Charles entered. He glared about him in annoyance and the stares—all except one—were averted. A thickset man in a blue suit seated at the back of the hall kept looking at him in a speculative, laconic way, refusing to be shamed into glancing away.

Charles's heart sank when he saw that the gathering was only a formal enquiry. No jury had been summoned so the verdict was to rest on the summing up of the coroner, a local tradesman with a face like one of the pigs' heads adorning his own shop window.

Proceedings opened with Sergeant Motherwell reciting his report. This was followed by Dr Spenser's medical findings, impressively couched in professional terms. The whole affair would have been wound up circumspectly with a homily from the butcher on the criminal carelessness of shooters in general and the reprehensible conduct of one in particular who, not only culpable of shooting out of season, was also the cause of this shocking accident, when Charles leapt to his feet.

"This is an absolute travesty!" he shouted, stammering slightly in his indignation. "I demand that further action be taken in order to find that person."

There was an excited stir among the people in the body of the hall, but the three men at the table on the platform did not seem surprised. Annoyed but resigned, they were expecting something like this. The coroner had been warned about Charles, so he was able to address him by name. He did so at first genially, as though Charles were a prospective customer crossing his sawdust threshold, then more austerely as he recalled his present role.

"I assure you, Mr Carmichael, that Sergeant Motherwell—ah—assures me that no stone will be left unturned, but—" he waved his podgy pink hand to the upturned faces, "with so many visitors swelling our community the task is a considerable one. For the present we can only pass our strongest censure on the cold-blooded person who does not see fit to come forward with abject apologies—"

"I don't want apologies," said Charles. "I want justice. Athol Sefton was not shot accidentally. He—"

"Mr Carmichael," interrupted the butcher loudly, who had also been warned of what Charles might say, "I must ask you to restrain yourself. I am sure you would not wish to make wild accusations in the heat of the moment, which I am—ah—sure you will regret later."

Charles swallowed. "Mr Coroner," he said in quieter tones, "I have no intention of making wild accusations, but in my opinion there is some sort of conspiracy afoot in order to keep me from uttering what I believe sincerely to be the truth. If you would allow me to bring certain matters to your attention—"

The coroner shook his porcine head. "Are these the same matters which I understand you brought to the attention of Sergeant Motherwell?"

"Er—yes, I suppose so. But the fool—I mean Sergeant Motherwell—"

"Then in that case, Mr Carmichael, I cannot allow you to continue. Furthermore, I would like to utter a word of warning." He consulted a sheet of paper on which he had written it in advance. "I understand your profession is that of—ah—editor and literary critic, and that the main type of fiction that you review is detective—ah—stories."

Charles closed his eyes as the butcher rambled on about making tolerant allowances because of his work and relationship to the deceased, but promising all sorts of dire penalties if he allowed his imagination to run away with him. "Won't any of you come forward to substantiate my beliefs?"

The coroner banged loudly on the table. "Mr Carmichael! I cannot permit you to behave in this unorthodox fashion. The enquiry is closed!" He got up quickly and left the platform with Dr Spenser and Sergeant Motherwell.

Charles slumped down in his place waiting for the hall to clear. Presently a chair scraped in the hollow emptiness and the last remaining spectator—the man in the blue suit—got up and advanced leisurely. Charles watched his approach sullenly.

Then the stranger spoke, a humorous inflection in his deep, deliberate voice. "What you need, boy, is a drink."

"I don't know who the hell you are," Charles told him slowly, "but I think you're right. Not one, but several drinks. Will you join me?"

"I'd be delighted. There's a pub just over the way."

They strolled out together, Charles with his hands in his pockets scowling at the ground, the other man stepping lightly and whistling tunelessly under his breath.

"Round one," he announced cheerfully, as they placed a foot each on the bar rung. "What'll it be?"

"Whisky and soda."

The stranger raised his eyebrow again and gave the order. "Beer for me."

They drank the first round in silence, Charles facing the counter with his left forearm resting on it, the other standing sideways with his glass in his hand.

"Round two," said Charles. "Repeat performance?"

The stranger nodded. "The name's McGrath."

"Delighted to know you, Mr McGrath. Carmichael is mine—as I suppose you heard back at that circus."

"You think there was a certain amount of hoop-holding?"

"You can say that again!"

"The coroner didn't let you say much. I gather you weren't in agreement with him?"

Charles drained his glass again and pushed it across the counter. He glanced around, then beckoned McGrath nearer. "Mustn't say it too loud, but the whole thing was a travesty."

"So you said back in the hall—way out loud. Why a travesty?"

"Because my uncle was murdered. Poor old Athol was deliberately and cold-bloodedly shot. Poor old Athol! Here's to him."

"Poor old Athol!" the other echoed gravely, raising his glass and lowering it again without drinking.

Charles leaned his other arm on the counter. "He was a great chap, Athol. A genius! And now he's dead. A genius one minute, then pouf! A corpse! A poor bloody corpse for a fool like Spenser to cut up. It was a privilege to know Athol. Did you know him?" he asked abruptly, turning his head and blinking McGrath into focus.

The other shook his head. "No, but as a matter of fact, I came here hoping to make his acquaintance."

"You did? You came to this damn awful place just to meet Athol?" A clouded thought eddied in Charles's mind which he tried to catch and clarify. "Are you a friend or foe?"

"Exactly what do you mean by that, Mr Carmichael?"

"I'll tell you in a minute. Wait for it!" He pondered for a moment, then said triumphantly, "Hah! I know what I meant. Did you come here to murder Athol?"

"No, I didn't come here to murder him. To be honest, I particularly wanted him alive."

Charles stared at him fixedly. "I believe you," he said at last. "I don't quite follow, but I believe you. Here, you're not drinking. I want to drink to you, Mr McGrath, because you're Athol's friend, and you didn't come to Dunbavin to murder him."

"Why, thanks. But I can hardly drink a toast to myself."

Charles nodded his head wisely and raised his glass. "True, very true. Here's to you, Mr McGrath. The only friend poor old Athol has." He pulled himself erect as he spoke and then lurched against McGrath. "I think I'd better sit down somewhere," he declared simply. He made careful progress to a bench in the corner.

"Athol has so few friends," he confided, when McGrath seated himself alongside. "Besides yourself, there is only me. But no one believes me, therefore I have no friends either. You see my reasoning?"

The other agreed amiably, and Charles went on sadly, "I thought Ellis would be my friend—but no, he wouldn't speak up for me. No one would come to my assistance. That is what friends are for—to come to your assistance when you want help. I feel very unhappy."

McGrath's eyes narrowed, hiding the watchful twinkle. "Perhaps I can offer my assistance, Mr Carmichael. What precisely is your trouble? Why wouldn't the people from the Duck and Dog come to your assistance?"

"Because they are afraid," said Charles aggressively, "and they have every reason to be. Do you think I'm going to allow Athol's murderer to go scot-free? Every one of them had a reason to dislike Athol, but one of them had a strong reason—strong enough to torment poor old Athol first before murdering him. I tried to tell Motherwell, but he wouldn't believe me. Margot knew he was a haunted and hunted man, but she wouldn't speak up with me either."

McGrath nodded his head soothingly like a confessor as he encouraged Charles to drool and muddle his way through the story. Charles thought he was marvellously understanding and kept breaking off to tell him so and how any friend of Athol's was a friend of his—how they must join forces to see justice done and Motherwell, Spenser and all the others at the Duck and Dog grovel. He also, somewhere during the discourse, begged McGrath—in view of their friendship through Athol—to call him Charles, and asked permission to call the other Mac since he did not know his right name. On being told it was Alexander, he begged to be allowed to continue with Mac, since he once knew a man called Alexander who used to split infinitives and drink nothing but straight gin.

McGrath agreed that in that case he would prefer Charles to call him Mac. In view of this step in their flourishing friendship he suggested that, as Charles wished him to join forces in seeking the truth of poor old Athol's death, it might be a good idea if he were to stay awhile at the Duck and Dog.

Charles swayed to his feet. "You can't know," he announced solemnly, "what it will mean to me to have a friend in that house of foes. Let us go at once and I will introduce you to Athol's murderers."

McGrath steered him out of the hotel. "Is that your car? I wonder if you would allow me to drive. I've got a sort of phobia about being driven."

"With the greatest pleasure on earth," said Charles, passing over the ignition key after much fumbling. "Do you know I think I'm a little drunk."

"Yes, you are a bit. I suggest you take a nap. I know the way to this place." He tucked Charles alongside the driver's seat and shut the door.

"All your suggestions are good ones," declared Charles. "First of all, the drinks. Then telling you about Athol and your coming to the Duck and Dog and now a nap. You're a very clever fellow, Mac."

"That remains to be seen," the other muttered, as he backed away from the kerb and set the car on the road.

IX

Charles's head was still lolling against the seat when McGrath pulled up outside the Duck and Dog.

"Come on, boy, wake up! Time for the introductions."

Charles stirred, opened hazy eyes, then closed them again and turned his head to the other side. McGrath grinned and got out of the car. He walked through the hotel, poking his head into rooms without encountering anyone until he reached the kitchen, where Miss Bryce was messily stuffing a pair of ducks.

Shelagh was in the dining room, setting the tables for dinner. The male voice brought her back to the kitchen. She thought it was Charles demanding lunch, and was ready to deliver a caustic lecture on guests who could not come to meals on time.

"Really most fortunate," Miss Bryce was saying, looking harassed when watching her hands trussing the birds and triumphant when she viewed McGrath. "Shelagh—here's someone for Mr Sefton's room. He is a friend of Mr Carmichael's. Isn't it lucky the way—my niece, Mr McGrath!"

"Where is Charles?" asked Shelagh sharply.

"Out in the car asleep."

"Asleep? Is he ill or something?"

"Something," McGrath returned imperturbably, giving her a quick scrutiny. "I'll take him up to his room if you will show me the way."

"Come along then." She led the way along the passage. "Are you really a friend of his? He didn't say anything about your coming to stay."

"You seem to be rather a sceptical young lady. Your aunt doesn't mind my staying."

"My aunt doesn't mind who comes as long as the rooms are full and the guests pay," said Shelagh crisply. "For myself, I think it is something of a coincidence that you should have known we had an unexpected vacancy."

"I've always been lucky," rejoined McGrath. "Hey, Charles! Wake up, will you, and set the young lady's mind at rest."

Charles opened his eyes. "Don't wanna—Lo Shee! Meet a friend of mine."

"You see?" said McGrath, "nothing hocus-pocus."

"I see that he is very drunk," she said warmly. "Come on, Chas, we'll help you up to your room."

"Feel foul!" he pronounced, making an effort to stay upright.

"I'll fix you some coffee and sandwiches presently. Whatever made you drink like that on an empty stomach?"

"She knows all about stomachs," Charles informed McGrath. "She's a nurse."

"Leave him be, Miss Bryce," said McGrath. "I can manage." He slung Charles across his shoulder and the girl led the way into the house and up the stairs.

"Don't make too much noise," she adjured, opening the bedroom door. "Everyone's having a sleep. They were up early this morning for the opening, then there was this inquest on Mr Sefton."

McGrath lowered his burden onto the bed. "I didn't see you there, Miss Bryce."

"I had better things to do," she replied crisply, unlacing Charles's shoes and covering him with a rug. She went to the door. "Your room is next to this one. I'll get someone to bring your bag up. The bathroom is two doors away. Dinner at 6:30."

"Just a minute, Miss Bryce!" He followed her out, shutting the door after him. "You seem an unusually cool and efficient girl. I'd like to have a chat with you."

"What about? I haven't a great deal of time."

"Is this my room? Don't you think you had better come and see if they've swept under the bed properly?"

"I did it myself this morning," she answered coldly.

"Well, come in anyway. I want to talk about our drunken young friend next door."

"It's not like Charles to get drunk. Why didn't you stop him instead of egging him on?"

"He acted like he had a grievance and seemed to find me understanding. I didn't want to spoil our beautiful new friendship."

"Well, I hope you didn't take too much notice of what he said. He's been behaving rather strangely since his uncle's death."

"He certainly told an interesting story. Do you think there might be something in it?"

The girl was silent. Presently she looked at him and asked quietly. "Who are you and where did you come from?"

"Sydney—the environs of Phillip Street. Do you know it?"

Her eyes flickered. "What brought you here? You're a long way off your—beat."

He gave a soft appreciative guffaw, then said, "I wanted to make the acquaintance of Mr Athol Sefton. It's very disconcerting to have come all this way—not to mention the difficulty I had in tracing him here—only to find that he has met with a fatal shooting accident."

"So you thought the next best thing to do would be to make Charles's acquaintance."

He nodded. "At least he can tell me something of what I missed—seems fond of his late uncle too. From what you say of them together, would you say that was so—or is Charles indulging in post-mortem affection?"

"They seemed to get on well enough," she replied shortly.

"You're not forthcoming, are you?"

"Look, Inspector or Sergeant or whatever you are, I don't know what business you wanted to discuss with Athol, but there has been enough disturbance here at the Duck and Dog already. Would you kindly not add to it!"

"Certainly," he replied promptly. "I'm only here to shoot ducks."

"That's what everyone's been saying," said Shelagh dryly and went out of the room.

Charles was sober when she returned sometime later with a tray of coffee and sandwiches, but looking as sickly as he declared himself to feel. "Do you want me to be really ill?" he demanded crossly, surveying the tray with distaste.

"You'll feel better when you've had something to eat," she said in a matter-of-fact voice. She poured out some coffee, put the cup into his hand and then sat on the end of the bed watching him.

"I wish you wouldn't look so virtuously healthy," grumbled Charles. "I know you're thinking what a poor weak fool I was getting tight over an inquest."

"I wasn't thinking anything like that. Drink up, then try a sandwich. I want to talk to you presently."

"What about?" he asked, picking over the plate of sandwiches half-heartedly.

"Your friend in the next room—Athol's room."

"What friend? Oh, you mean that chap who drove me home. Mac something."

"McGrath. Do you know he's a detective? He came all the way from Sydney in order to see Athol."

"Yes, I remember he mentioned something, but I didn't know he was a cop. How did you find that out?"

"He told me. Have another sandwich!"

"I wish you'd stop the ministering angel stuff."

"I merely want to make you sufficiently strong so as to tell your friend to leave," she replied, taking his cup and refilling it.

"I'm not going to tell him to leave," said Charles truculently. "In fact, I'm damned glad I got tight and invited him here. I remember now I told him all about Athol's murder. He must think I have something and wants to look over the suspects for himself."

His jubilant train of thought was interrupted by a knock at the door. Shelagh got up and opened it. "I thought I heard voices," said McGrath. "May I come in?"

"Come right in," Charles invited jovially. "It's nice to see only one of you for a change."

McGrath laughed. "How do you feel now?"

"Fair enough. Shelagh tells me you're a detective from Sydney town."

"You didn't say not to tell him," the girl interpolated.

"Well, you'd better not tell anyone else, Shelagh, please," said Charles. "The quieter we keep Mac's identity the better. I might as well admit having thrown my weight about too much over this business. Now that fool Motherwell is on my wheel, I'm going to move along more quietly. Mac can handle things here."

"What things might they be?" enquired McGrath politely. "My business in Dunbavin has nothing to do with Miss Bryce's guests."

Charles stared at him. "What are you talking about? Someone here murdered Athol—you know, my uncle, Athol Sefton."

"So you said earlier. Don't think I'm not interested, boy, but I'm the sort of bloke who likes to do one thing at a time. I was sent here on a certain assignment, and until I've cleaned that up, your uncle's death is not my immediate concern—if, indeed, it ever will be."

Charles, who had sat up when the detective entered, sank back with a grin and closed his eyes. "I'm having a relapse."

"What is this certain assignment?" said Shelagh.

"Rather a delicate job—even more so now. I was sent to investigate a suspected case of murder."

Charles opened his eyes again. "Now you're talking sense and I can follow you."

"Don't speak too soon," warned Shelagh. "I don't see how Mr McGrath was sent on Athol's account if he didn't know he was dead until he arrived in Dunbavin."

"Don't try being tortuous too," Charles implored. "My head won't stand it."

"I'm not being tortuous. It's obvious Mr McGrath is here to investigate someone else's death—not Athol's."

"Then where does Athol come in? Why did you want to see him so particularly? You can't mean Athol murdered someone!"

McGrath gazed at him blankly. "That is being rather blunt. Let's say I wanted to ask your uncle a few questions."

Charles stared back at him in a bemused fashion, then turned to the girl. "More coffee, Shelagh," he begged. She refilled his cup and presently he said more briskly, "Let's put all the cards on the table and cut out the delicacy. Athol is suspected of murder. Now he has been murdered—Oh yes, he has, Shelagh, so stop looking shocked—therefore you are now after a double murderer. Whom do you suspect now?"

"Your line of reasoning is not altogether accurate," began McGrath.

"Oh, stop playing around the point. You must have someone in mind."

"All right," said McGrath serenely. "You."

"What!" Charles jerked upright and swung his legs off the bed. "I've never murdered anyone in my life. And I certainly couldn't have shot Athol. The range was over a hundred yards and I was right alongside. Where the deuce are my shoes? Shelagh, I suppose you took them off."

"I warned you my job has become even more delicate," McGrath said righteously.

"Delicate be—Oh, thanks!" he broke off as the girl gave him his shoes, and sat on the bed to tug them on furiously. "I've never heard such bloody impertinence in my life. Suspecting me of killing my own uncle!"

"Charles, behave yourself!"

He swung round on her. "I bet you're as pleased as punch over this. Nothing delights you more than making me look a fool."

McGrath lowered himself into a chair with an air of one waiting for the storm to subside. "No one's making you look a fool," said the girl cuttingly. "And far from being pleased, I wish you'd be quiet and allow Mr McGrath to explain further."

"You're a sensible girl, Miss Bryce."

"She's too damned sensible," Charles growled. "She's never likely to find herself accused of double murder. And you, Mac! To think that I drank with you, that I thought you were understanding and all the time—Oh, it beats all. Athol wouldn't have been so taken in."

"Probably not," agreed McGrath laconically. "A man with a guilty conscience is usually on his guard."

"Why, Charles!" Shelagh touched his arm suddenly. "That's what was wrong with Athol—a guilty conscience."

"Athol didn't have any sort of conscience at any time. It was those threatening notes and telephone calls that were worrying him. The person he is alleged to have murdered could hardly have had anything to do with them."

"You told me someone said he seemed haunted," suggested McGrath helpfully.

Charles shot him a kindling glance. "That was Margot Stainsbury, and according to her Athol asked if she believed in ghosts too! I flatly refuse to have the supernatural obtruding. There's been enough breaking of the rules of the game as it is. Vengeful ghosts would be the ruddy limit."

"He's a disciple of the detective story," explained Shelagh scornfully.

"Then I see I'll have my work cut out," replied McGrath in genial tones.

"Stop suggesting that I'm a murderer. I don't even know who I'm supposed to have killed, anyway. Produce your body."

"Well, that is a little difficult."

"What! No body? Did I dissolve it in an acid bath?"

"No—but your uncle Athol Sefton had it cremated."

All his angry flippancy dropped away from Charles. He sank slowly onto the bed staring at McGrath, who returned his gaze unblinkingly. After a moment's silence he said in a subdued voice, "You mean his wife? My aunt Paula?"

The other nodded.

"I see!" said Charles heavily.

The detective shifted in his chair. "One has to proceed very carefully in cases like these. Mrs Sefton has been dead for some time. I understand that she was more or less an invalid, suffering from some peculiar debility."

"Peculiar debility is right! I was fond of my aunt—after all, she was a blood relation whereas Athol was not—but I always had the idea that she took to her invalid bed for want of something better to do. Athol was neither a kind man nor an attentive husband. Her pills and her potions and her Macquarie Street specialists were all she had in life."

Shelagh nodded professionally. "Wealthy lonely women often develop hypochondriacal tendencies."

"What happened?" Charles asked the detective. "Why has so much time been allowed to lapse before this enquiry?"

"If the doctor in attendance signs the necessary certificate of death, there is not much to be done. According to him your aunt died of heart failure brought on by acute gastritis, which in turn was the result of years of punishing her organs with various patent medicines."

"But you think she was poisoned," said Charles bluntly.

"Yes, it's possible that she was," agreed McGrath coolly. "It's certainly what two or three busy-bodies seem to think. Some acquaintances of your aunt felt it their public duty to bring to the notice of the police that your aunt was a wealthy, neglected wife, that Athol Sefton was too good-looking and charming to be trusted, that she had often spoken with regret of the money she had sunk in that classy magazine he produced, and lastly that she had been heard to say she preferred burial to cremation and had a vault already prepared to receive her remains."

"Yes, I knew that. I often wondered why Athol had her cremated. Go on!"

"That's about all there is. My job now is either to shut the busy-bodies up or to prove foul play."

"And now that Athol isn't around you intend to pin Aunt Paula's death on me!"

"Oh, I wouldn't go so far as that—yet!" returned McGrath cheerfully. "Let's say that the questions I intended asking your uncle will now be transferred to you as the—er—next interested party."

"I neither shot Athol nor poisoned my aunt," said Charles emphatically. "I've told you why the first is impossible. As for Paula—I haven't even been in Sydney for a year."

"Thirteen months," corrected the detective.

Charles gasped. "You mean you've already checked on me?"

"The busy-bodies mentioned your name, though they admitted your aunt seemed fond of you, and quite devoted you were in little attentions—like sending her special chocolates from Melbourne."

"That's right," said Charles eagerly. "I told you I was also fond—" He broke off and stared at the other suspiciously. McGrath's laconic eye-brow was up. "Oh, I get it," he said bitterly. "You think I loaded the chocolates with arsenic."

"I can see this young fellow is going to be a lot of help to me," McGrath remarked to Shelagh conversationally.

"I think Charles had better help himself first."

"That's just what I mean. If he doesn't want to face a double-murder charge, he had better do something pretty fast."

"And while I do all the work you're going to hang around looking on—is that it?" asked Charles.

"Yes, that's it," returned McGrath equably. "A cushy job, after all."

Shelagh looked from one to the other with folded lips. Then she made a sound of exasperation, picked up the tray and went out of the room. "Attractive girl!" McGrath vouchsafed after the door had been banged rather than closed. "Seems rather interested in you too. Doesn't seem the type to be emoting for nothing."

"I suggest," said Charles coldly, "that you keep your revolting innuendos to the subject of murder. Are you really serious about leaving the job of investigation to me?"

"Depends which job you mean. As far as mine is concerned, I could wrap the whole thing up right now. But if your uncle was murdered, then you can't blame me for having unkind thoughts. We're simple, direct sort of blokes, we coppers. If a wealthy woman dies in suspicious circumstances, we just turn naturally to the husband to ask questions. If there is no husband, the nearest relative does just as nicely."

"Well, I'm damned if I will back down now and say Athol was not murdered. Okay—I'll do what I can, but you've got to play fair, Mac. I don't know how serious you are when you say you suspect me, but there's to be no prejudice."

"Fair enough," the other agreed amiably. "Go to it, boy!"

X

Dinner that night was quite a lively meal. There was an air of tacit celebration about it. What with the good bags obtained at the opening of the season and the result of the inquest, everyone felt at temporary peace with each other. Even Charles's past behaviour was overlooked, with Mrs Dougall setting the example by addressing him with gracious condescension.

McGrath was accepted without curiosity as someone who had heard by chance that there was a free room at the Duck and Dog. Only Ellis showed any signs of scepticism, making one or two of those quizzical little remarks with which he liked to prove his awareness of anything unusual. "Quite a happy coincidence!" he remarked when McGrath was introduced, "but we don't hold with coincidences, do we, Charles? Quite against the rules!"

"What rules?" asked McGrath stolidly. He was presenting an amiable, ox-like front to the company which Charles secretly applauded—especially when Ellis's bland barbs fell short. At first he wondered if Shelagh had told her father of the new guest's identity, but a hurried consultation with her at the servery window reassured him. In fact, she gave the impression that Charles's affairs were of less moment than the exact timing of adding a glass of port to the ducks cooked 'en casserole'.

"I had the misfortune to be waylaid this morning by our good doctor's wife," Ellis announced presently. "A truly redoubtable woman! She held me transfixed until she extracted my promise to attend some arty-crafty tea party she is conducting tomorrow."

"What do you mean—arty-crafty?" demanded Mrs Dougall with a booming, slightly self-conscious laugh. "I met Mrs Spenser too. She wants me to give her guests a talk on some of our Indian experiences. One must do one's bit, you know."

"So long as it's only a bit," murmured Ellis as he turned to Charles. "The things that woman made me promise! She talked down any objections I had before I could even produce them. I found myself finally suggesting all sorts of items to help her wretched soirée, or whatever it is. You, Charles, are to give a talk—your presence here delights her more than it does her spouse. What have you done to offend our medico, I wonder? Of course, it is most regrettable that Mrs Spenser is not able to capture a greater literary lion. She tried so hard on past occasions with your poor Athol. The naughty fellow was quite brutal in his snubs, so do be complaisant like a good chap." He switched his mocking gaze to McGrath, who was enjoying his dinner solemnly, apparently impervious to his surroundings. "And our latest acquisition to the Duck and Dog! Such a pity that time will not allow us to discover some latent talent which I feel sure lurks behind that phlegmatic exterior—eh, Mr McGrath?"

The detective merely grinned politely and went on masticating.

"Ellis smells something," Charles muttered in McGrath's ear as they left the dining room. "Trust him! Look, I'm going to get out of the way. They won't loosen up while I'm around. This is also a good opportunity to reconnoitre. I want to find that missing Wilding."

On his way upstairs he met Margot, who had slipped up to her room to do some after-dinner facial reconstruction. "Darling! Long time, no see! Such a messy day for you, poor sweet. They tell me you got boozed."

"That's right," he said wanly. "And now I'm paying for it. Shocking head, so I thought I'd pile in early. Are you going shooting tomorrow?"

She gave a shudder of revulsion. "Never again! I had no idea such early hours existed, except, of course, from the other end. And they do it for fun!"

"Well, don't let me detain you. Your new beau is waiting for you."

She smiled complacently. "Harry? Isn't he a lamb!"

"Jerry seems to consider him more of a wolf. You'd better watch out."

"Oh—Jerry! I can manage him. By the way, who's your new chum?"

"McGrath? Just someone I got talking to at the pub in the township. What do you think of him?"

"Well, dear, I don't want to sound rude, but if he's not a particular friend of yours I'd vote him a little heavy. Good-night, poor Chas." She gave him a quick butterfly kiss. "I won't let them say too many nasty things about you, but you have been an awful ass, haven't you."

"I suppose I have," he agreed humbly. He watched her synthetically graceful figure disappear down the stairs, waited a few seconds and then quietly entered her room. After one quick comprehensive glance round, he set about a systematic and thorough search. Soon he had made a neat survey of the whole room with which, although unrewarding, he felt satisfied as a testing ground. But when several other rooms proved equally fruitless, he began to wonder if he were not behaving like those meddling heroines he deplored in books.

Putting himself in the place of the murderer, Charles could not believe that the Wilding rifle had been thrown away haphazardly into the bush where sooner or later someone would come across it. Far better to hang on to it, and do the throwing away as far from the scene of the crime as possible. Convinced that the person he was up against, who had been so careful and clever in planning Athol's death, would not make a blunder over the disposal of the weapon, he patiently and painstakingly poked away at beds and pried into cupboards.

The monotony of his search was broken in Harris Jeffery's room, where he came upon three items of interest. The first was a Luger revolver hanging in a shoulder holster in the wardrobe, but the edge was taken off this discovery by his recalling Wilson making some mention of it. The other two items were contained in an old shagreen wallet which had been slipped into one of the compartments of an airlines carry-all.

One was a receipted account for services rendered by 'Dawson and Stanley, Private Enquiry Agents', the other a worn and creased letter which bore a Sydney suburban address and was dated June 1943. He read it quickly, despising his own meddling.

'Harry—if you ever set foot in this country again I'll beat you to pulp, so help me! You Yanks came over here to help us beat the Nips, not to see how many of our women you could ruin. We thought we could trust you. Barbie swore she could and was always ticking us off if we said anything about you. You skunk—taking advantage of a girl like my sister. Why she couldn't tell Mum and me instead of doing what she did, we can't work out. She was always a good kid, too. I bet you put her up to it. She had a lot of pain before she died, but she still would not let anyone say a word against you. I hope the thought of that gives you all the hell you deserve, you mongrel!' It was signed 'Mick'.

Charles made a face of distaste and put the letter back carefully. Was it because of this letter that Jeffrey had come back to Australia? With such a threat hanging over him, it seemed hard to believe. And for what reason had Jeffrey employed the services of a private enquiry agent? Shrugging in a puzzled way, Charles put the room to rights and went out.

He had spent quite a considerable time going over the American's belongings, but there remained only one more room to search— Adelaide Dougall's. This was comparatively simple for Adelaide's belongings were meagre. There was still no sign of the missing Wilding and by now Charles had given up hope of finding it in the house. He planned a search of the hotel environs in the morning.

In a drawer of Adelaide's dressing-table, he came across a folio of loose sheets written over in a round unformed hand and paused to glance through her literary efforts. He decided that if they were worth anything, he might do something about getting them published in order to make up a bit for Athol's beastliness to the poor woman. He read through a couple of stories objectively, then shook his head. The last story in the folder was unfinished. Adelaide must have been writing it only recently. Giving her every chance, he began to read.

Presently he raised his head, bundled the folder back into the drawer and hurried out of the room. There was just time to get inside his own door when the other guests came trooping upstairs to bed.

"Hey, Mac!" he called softly as the detective passed.

"Yes, what do you want?"

Charles pulled him in and shut the door, saying indignantly, "You don't mean to say you were going to bed without conferring!"

"Well, I was," admitted McGrath dampingly. "It's nearly eleven and I'm booked to shoot ducks at dawn. What do you want to confer about?"

"What do I want—? Well, that's rich, that is! I want to know if you picked up anything. I haven't been inactive up here."

"Haven't you?" asked McGrath, surveying Charles's pyjamas laid out on the bed with a bedazzled eye.

"Well, what do you think of them?"

"Who? Oh, the other guests? They seem the usual amiable assortment you find at any country pub."

"Did they talk about Athol or me?"

"You were both mentioned now I come to think of it."

"What was said? Come on, man! What's the matter with you?"

"Maybe it's those stripes of yours. Cover them up, will you, before I develop a tic."

"Oh, don't talk rot," said Charles in disgust. "Listen, I managed to search the bedrooms. I think I know why that American chap has something on his mind. Did you know he's toting a Luger? Then there's the Dougall girl. She writes stories. I read one that she must have started after Athol disillusioned her—you never saw so much vitriol. I'd say she had it in her to kill him."

McGrath rubbed his chin. "That the dowdy woman with the glittering eye? Looks a bit round the bend?" Charles nodded. "And she can shoot too. The three of them can. If only I could find that bloody rifle. Come on, Mac, bend your brain. Where would you hide a stolen rifle?"

"Why ask me?" the other drawled. "You should know."

Charles gazed at him blankly before light dawned. "Oh, you are not still on that tack, are you? You know damn well I didn't even want to shoot Athol like some of the others around here."

"I don't know anything damn well," returned McGrath amiably, "but it's nice to know you're trying to dig up information to clear yourself. Keep it up, boy. Do you mind if I push off now? I'd like to be fairly fresh for the sport tomorrow."

"If you happen to get shot," said Charles roundly, "it will be your just deserts and I won't lift a finger to do anything."

"Oh, I don't think that's likely to happen. After all, you won't be there." McGrath caught the pillow Charles threw at his head, returned it deftly and went out.

Charles's emotional state after this encounter was not conducive to sound slumber. He spent part of the night lying awake apostrophising with eloquent invective McGrath, Athol, Shelagh and anyone else whose mental image came before him. In a vain effort to atrophy his feelings, he turned over the review books belonging to Athol. But when he read on one of the publisher's slips a message which ran 'Pan this, Athol, and I'll shoot you!' He threw them to the floor, slumped on his bed and groaned loudly and unheedingly.

From this lonely pastime, he was aroused by a light knock at the door. A happier gleam came into his eye and he sat up. "Who is it?"

A soft voice said anxiously, "It's Frances Turner. Are you all right, Mr Carmichael? I thought I heard you call out."

"You can come in. I was groaning, not calling out."

She put her head in, surveying him doubtfully. "Are you ill? Is there anything I can do?"

Her air of concern was easy on Charles's jaundiced gaze and wounded spirit. "No, there's nothing you can do. I can't sleep, that's all."

"Oh, how wretched!" she exclaimed in a whisper. "Have you—"

"Yes, I've tried a sedative, reading and counting sheep. I'm sorry to have disturbed you. Please go back to bed."

She cast an anxious look over her shoulder. "Andy's got some special sleeping tablets. Let me get you a couple."

"They're certain to have no effect on me," said Charles in martyred accents. "So please don't bother. I'll just lie here and wait for the dawn."

She smiled a little. "It's quite a wait. You might as well try them. Andy has made me take them before this and they're marvellous. I'll be back in a moment."

She returned presently carrying a tumbler of water. "Here they are! Swallow them down and let me straighten your bed."

"Very good of you," Charles mumbled as he gulped.

"That's all right. I know what it's like not being able to sleep." She pulled and tucked deftly and thumped up his pillows, her face grave and kind.

Charles suddenly knew how it was patients so often fell in love with their nurses. A certain type of nurse, he thought darkly, remembering Shelagh. "That's just wonderful!" he announced, as she smoothed the sheet under his chin, then stood surveying him as though she'd like to find more to do. "Were you a nurse, by any chance?"

She shook her head. "No, but I looked after my invalid sister for many years. You can't help finding out how to make people comfortable. Now you just relax and I'm sure you'll drop off soon."

"Andy's a very lucky man," said Charles.

She turned back from the door, smiling shyly at the compliment. She then said seriously, "Don't think worrying thoughts. It's worry that keeps you awake—and bad memories. Good-night!"

"Good-night!" echoed Charles. What a nice little woman, he thought, putting out a hand to switch off the lights. Too bad that lout will never appreciate her. Such a nice, understanding, womanly, little—Charles rolled over and fell fast asleep.

XI

The strident sound of a car engine with an open throttle taking the rise up to the hotel awakened Charles the next morning. He got up and went to the window. Ellis had planned to conduct his guests further afield than Teal Lagoon. The ducks had been frightened away from there and it would be some days before the decoys would coax them back again. Charles dimly remembered hearing the departure of the party in the Bryce station wagon.

Presently the Turners' utility came into view, driven by Ellis with Jerry alongside. It drew up under Charles's window. "Is anything the matter?" he called sharply, as Ellis opened Jerry's door and proceeded to help him out.

Ellis looked up. "The very person I want to see! Come on down, my dear fellow."

Charles hurried on his dressing-gown and went downstairs. The Bryces were in the hall, Jerry with one arm supported by his other hand. There was blood on the upper sleeve of his yellow pullover and he looked more than ordinarily stormy.

"He got into someone's range of fire," explained Ellis. "Just a graze or two—nothing serious—but such a coincidence, don't you agree, Charles? Do you know, I have the oddest feeling that here, but for a quirk of fate, am I."

"I wish you'd stop talking and help me out of this," said Jerry, trying to ease his way out of his pullover.

"You render assistance, Charles. I'll go and find Shelagh. An admirable girl in crisis. The sight of blood may turn some people squeamish, but to my daughter it is a challenge."

"He's been talking like that all the way back," said Jerry. "We left the station wagon for the others."

"What on earth possessed you to get ahead of the guns?"

"I didn't get ahead," he returned indignantly. "We were all spread around the Upper Lagoon. That fool Dougall's idea—he said we'd bag more if we separated."

"Then you don't know who did it?"

"If I knew that," declared Jerry roundly, "I'd be peppering someone's backside right now."

"Shelagh's coming," announced Ellis, coming back, "plus a bowl of water and a dozen other accoutrements. My poor Jerry, what an unpleasant mess! I must say I'm glad you were so insistent on my handing over your pullover. Never mind, you can wear a sling and Margot will change the range of her gaze. I understand slings have the most devastating effect on females."

"Was the pullover exchange the quirk of fate?" asked Charles.

"How acute you are!" Ellis marvelled. "I was only saying so to our stolid friend McGrath last night; hoping, of course, to inspire a little acuteness into him. That unwinking solemnity and so slow to reply! I tried every way I could to shock him into natural behaviour—even hinting broadly that I agreed with you about Athol's accident and that, should the effort not be so tedious, it would be well in my powers to find the person who killed him."

Charles gave him a withering glance. "You were a fool to talk like that. Don't you realise what could have happened—what might happen yet?"

"And I thought you'd be grateful," said Ellis plaintively. "Admittedly I dislike the idea of being a clay pigeon, but it does help to clarify the position for you."

"I don't need anything clarified."

"No, but your friend Mr McGrath might," said Ellis gently.

"Well, let this be a warning to you," said Charles, pointing to Jerry.

"I think that is all it was meant to be," Ellis reflected. "Long range and a shotgun. You can't expect to do the same damage as with—let's say—a Wilding."

"Well, I'm damned glad it wasn't a Wilding," protested Jerry, outraged. "I might have been killed."

"The thought of such a possibility, my son, appals me," said Ellis kindly. "Ah, here is your sister, come to put everything to rights and everyone in their places!"

"I'm going upstairs to get dressed," said Charles, suddenly conscious of his unshaven, dishevelled state.

As Ellis had predicted, Margot fussed prettily over Jerry at breakfast, cutting his toast and decapitating his boiled egg. Shelagh had ordered him to Dr Spenser's morning surgery for a check up on her work which she knew was an unnecessary precaution, and McGrath had offered to escort him.

"You're not running out on me, are you?" Charles asked suspiciously, waylaying the detective in the hall.

"What a thought!" exclaimed McGrath virtuously. "I have a good mind not to ask for a loan of your car. You look like Sunday's leftovers, boy! Anything troubling you?"

"Oh, no, not a thing! Here I am, sweating my insides out trying to solve a murder which you think I committed and which no one else thinks happened, and you go off with Jerry to hold his hand."

McGrath grinned. "Perhaps if you'd come out with the party this morning, it might have been your hand."

Charles's expression changed quickly. "What did you make of the shooting? Ellis thinks it was intended as a warning to him."

"A very whimsical character is Mr Bryce," said the other, not committing himself. "Well, I'd better collect the patient and make tracks. Want me to do anything for you in the township?"

"Nothing, thanks—but I'd still like to know why you're escorting Jerry."

"Just out of the kindness of my heart—plus the fact that there are one or two commissions I have to perform."

"Commissions for whom?"

"You, boy! By the way, you don't happen to have that bullet on you—the one that killed your uncle?"

Charles stared at him wonderingly. "I have it right here. Why do you want it?"

"Thanks." McGrath slipped it into his pocket casually and turned to go.

Charles caught him by the arm. "Come on, Mac," he said coaxingly. "What are you going to do with that bullet?"

"Send it down to Melbourne for a ballistics report."

"What sort of report can they give without the gun that fired it?"

"Oh, I'm sending that along too," returned the detective easily.

Charles choked. "You—where—?"

"Now, take it easy, boy!"

Charles found his voice. "Where did you discover it and why didn't you tell me? You know damned well how much finding that Wilding means to me."

McGrath cocked an eyebrow. "I told you before, boy, I don't know anything damned well."

"When and where?" Charles demanded in a pent-up voice.

"This morning—under the front seat of your car."

"Yes, I was going to search the cars this morn—what did you say? My car?"

"You seem amazed," observed McGrath coolly.

Charles mouthed and waved his hands like Wilson in one of his spasms while the detective watched him with a detached interest. "A plant!" he pronounced at last.

"I rather expected you to say that," McGrath said maddeningly.

"Now, look here, Mac—I know what you're thinking, or rather what you're pretending to think, but I had no idea that bloody gun was in my car. Absolutely no idea! Is that clear?"

"Whatever you say, boy, but you don't mind if I have my own ideas on the subject."

Charles groaned in despair. "I give up. I'll shoot myself and leave a letter explaining all."

McGrath chuckled. "Oh, don't do that. The game's never lost until it's won, or should that be the other way round?"

"The way you're playing it, the game's to the killer. I looked for help from you, Mac not hindrance."

"I'm not hindering you. You keep on going right ahead."

"Okay, I will," snapped Charles. "I'll find the person who killed Athol and shot at Ellis this morning, if it's the last thing I do."

XII

It was a bright fine morning and the guests had wandered outside to blink and idle in the sun, leaving the house free for Miss Bryce and Shelagh to tear purposefully through their work. Their energy had inspired Ellis into taking refuge in the bar where he was conducting a desultory stocktaking.

Mrs Dougall's platform tones reached Charles's ears first—". . . a full moon and just a faint breeze, enough to carry the scent of the prey. Conditions were ideal. Ah, Mr Carmichael, good morning! I was running through the drill for this afternoon. As a literary man, you must tell me what you think of it."

"One of these days you really must write your memoirs, my dear," said Major Dougall, his eyes bulging sycophantically. "I'll never forget that tiger shoot, and you describe it so well that it seems only yesterday."

"I'd rather you described this morning's duck-shoot," said Charles.

The major looked at him as though he had mentioned the blockage in the local sewer. "Disgraceful business! Can't think what people are coming to nowadays."

Mrs Dougall looked at Charles full in the eye. "Lamentable carelessness, but an accident, of course."

"Oh, without doubt an accident. Is it tactless to enquire if anyone knows who was responsible?"

"No one knows and no one wishes to know," said Mrs Dougall severely.

"Then I take it you don't intend to lose sleep over the incident."

Before his wife could engage the enemy, Major Dougall broke in with an affable choke. "Nothing ever disturbs my wife's slumber. Remember that time in Bombay, my dear? We were staying at the Taj and a thief got into our room. I woke up, grabbed him and called the police, but you slept through the whole thing."

"How very interesting!" said Charles politely. "You must include the story in your memoirs, Mrs Dougall."

He strolled across to where Margot was lounging with careful grace in a cane chaise-lounge and turning over the pages of a fashion magazine in which her own countenance appeared several times. Wilson was hovering about her adoringly.

"Is that the best you can do?" Charles asked, after she had got rid of him with charming dexterity.

"Funny little man! I find him rather touching."

"Where's Harris P. Jeffrey?" asked Charles, taking the magazine from her and flipping over the pages.

"Oh, somewhere around. Not playing because I petted Jerry at breakfast."

"Another day or so when Jerry discards the romantic sling, you'll discard him."

"What a beast you are when you try to imitate Athol!"

"Jerry was closer to being an imitation."

She gave him one of her wide glances, then shivered. "Don't Charles! I knew you'd try to make something out of this morning's shooting, but please don't. You won't get anywhere."

He regarded her closely for a moment, then asked, "You knew my aunt Paula, didn't you?"

"Slightly," she agreed cautiously.

"What would you say if I told you that there is a suspicion that she did not die naturally—that Athol might have poisoned her?"

She took a deep breath and sat up tensely. "I'd say I'm not surprised. You know, Chas, it passed through my mind at the time— what I mean is, a man like Athol and her! She was a dreadful drear, you know, and she held the purse strings. A ghastly thing, but you really can't blame Athol, can you?"

Her unconscious callousness sent a wild theory through his mind. Supposing it had been Margot who had poisoned Mrs Sefton. He remembered his suspicion that she was trying to get Athol to marry her. Supposing that when she realised that Athol had no intention of falling in with her plans . . . He glanced down at the slim scarlet-tipped hand resting carelessly on his.

"What are you thinking about?" she asked, meeting his gaze limpidly.

He got up, dropping the magazine onto her lap. "Not nice thoughts. Shall I call Wilson back? I rather want to have a talk with Harry Jeffrey before you besot him again."

He left her and went round the side of the hotel towards the garages. The Turners' utility was standing outside. Andrew had his head under the raised bonnet, revving up the engine, while Frances, with a little frown of concentration on her face, was making a neat job of packing their belongings in the back.

"Are you leaving us?" asked Charles.

She looked up with a start. "Oh—Mr Carmichael! Yes, we're moving on. Andy—that is, we only planned to stay a short time." She paused, glanced at her husband's back view, then said hesitantly, "I suppose it's all right our going?"

"Quite all right," said Charles, smiling. "Here, let me lift that bag for you!"

"Thank you. Did you manage to get to sleep?"

"I did—thanks to you."

"Then—then everything is all right?"

"Hey, Frankie! Switch off, will you?" called Turner.

"Everything is all right as far as you're concerned. When you leave you can forget a place called Dunbavin ever existed. I'm only sorry your honeymoon was so marred."

"I won't forget you," she said, breathlessly. "You've been—I'm sorry, Andy, I'm coming!"

Turner put the bonnet down with a bang and wiped his hands on a piece of rag. "What do you want?" he asked Charles truculently.

"Just to say good-bye and good luck and—happier hunting elsewhere."

"Oh—thanks! But we're not pushing off at once. Frankie's keen to go to this afternoon social in the town. I thought we'd take it in on our way."

"I'm not a bit keen," the girl protested. "Really, dear, I'd be quite happy to carry straight on."

"We were asked to do it, weren't we? Bryce said the invitation included everyone staying here. Okay, that's us. We go—and my wife is going to knock the spots off the rest of them, Mr Carmichael."

"Oh, are you going to contribute something?"

"I don't want to," she said, with another fleeting glance at her husband. "You see, back home I used to do a little acting. Very amateurish I know, but—"

"Don't you take any notice of her," interrupted Andrew. "She's hot stuff. I've seen them laid in the aisles when she puts on a funny sketch."

"Oh, Andy!" she said deprecatingly. "What are you going to do, Mr Carmichael? Mr Bryce said some sort of lecture."

"Er—yes. It's just a little talk I've given before on the detective novel."

"That should be very interesting," she said politely.

"Mrs Dougall is giving a talk too," said Charles, nettled by the blank look on Andrew's face. "A tiger shoot in India."

"Now that should be pretty good," he said enthusiastically. "I've always wanted to shoot big game. I guess hearing about it will be the next best."

"Well, I'll let you get on with your packing. By the way, this morning's accident to Jerry—you don't know how it happened, do you?"

There was a short pause before Andrew replied, "No, we don't. Come on, Frankie! Help get the tarpaulin on. Cheer-oh, Mr Carmichael!"

Charles looked at the girl, but she seemed to avoid his eyes. With a puzzled frown he moved away.

He ran the American to earth in the lounge and without preamble said, "I want to ask you a couple of questions."

Jeffrey pulled a packet of cigarettes from a pocket and flipped one up. "You sure are a persistent guy. I'm not going to act dumb and pretend I don't know what you want to talk about. You still think someone shot your uncle, don't you?"

"Yes, I do. Do you mind?"

"Why should I mind? It's nothing to do with me. Remember I never met Sefton before Saturday night."

"The continual reminder makes me doubtful on that point. I understand you have a Luger revolver. I'm not interested in how it got past our Customs, but just why did you bring it on a duck-shooting expedition?"

"I didn't know how strict your hunting authorities were here."

"Meaning that in the States you are permitted to shoot wild-fowl with any sort of firearm?"

"I can't say—that is—"

"No, you can't say!" Charles cut in. "And do you know why, Mr Jeffrey? I don't think you've ever been duck-shooting before. Ellis Bryce spotted that at once."

"Yes, it was quite smart of me," agreed Ellis, coming into the room laden with various bottles and glasses. "The bar is what can only be termed a shambles. Shelagh has just been in to tell me that I have bitten off more than I can chew, so I thought I'd come in here and try drinking more than I can swallow instead. Do help yourself to whatever you can find, and tell me what progress you have been making, my poor Charles. From the baffled expression on your face and the distinctly guarded one on Mr Jeffrey's I should say no progress at all. I feel almost constrained to render you further assistance."

"Very good of you," said Charles dryly. "I don't doubt your ability, Ellis, merely your methods. And remember Jerry won't be always around to exchange pullovers."

"Charles is not a bit grateful to me for playing clay pigeon this morning," Ellis complained to the American. "My idea—I get these extraordinary flashes of genius—was to make you come out into the open, to force you into declaring yourself, so to speak."

XIII

The American rose slowly from his chair. "Say, wait a minute! What do you mean—make me come into the open? I didn't shoot at Jerry this morning."

Ellis regarded him blandly. "You didn't? You're absolutely sure of that?"

"Dead sure!" snapped Jeffrey.

"What an apt epithet! Charles, why are you goggling in that foolish way? Do give Mr Jeffrey a drink. He seems a trifle distracted."

"I'm not surprised," replied Charles, finding his voice.

"Okay Bryce! Cut the funny stuff and let's have it. So you think I shot Jerry in mistake for you. I suppose that's because you were shooting off your mouth last night about discovering Sefton's killer. You think you're so damn clever, but you seem to forget I never met Sefton before three days ago. Why should I want to kill a perfect stranger?"

Ellis eyed him critically. "It is evident even to an average intelligence that your insistence that you and Athol were perfect strangers is a shade too insistent. I'm surprised that Charles has taken so long to bypass the obstacle. I think the connection between you was a mutual acquaintance. Athol may not have known you, but you knew of him very well indeed."

"Is he right, Jeffrey?"

"My dear Charles, of course I'm right. I'm never wrong in anything to which I bend my brain. There's no use looking for corroboration from Mr Jeffrey. He won't give it and I find your attitude an insult."

"I'm not talking—yet," said the American grimly. "Go on, Bryce."

"The mutual acquaintance was, I should say, a woman. Knowing Athol, that goes without saying, don't you agree, Charles?"

Out of the corner of his eye, Charles saw Jeffrey's hand tighten on the glass he held. "It is possible," he agreed briefly.

"Now, there were three types of women Athol dabbled in. There was the willing victim, the sophisticated dodger—the charming Margot once belonged to that group—and lastly the foolishly innocent. From my observance of Mr Jeffrey, I should say that the female who formed the connection between him and Athol belonged to the last group. I trust you can follow me, Charles?"

"Quite easily. You are about to suggest that Jeffrey's motive for murdering Athol was revenge for wronging a girl he was in love with."

Ellis made a moue of distaste. "You think such a conclusion unworthy of me? Commonplace though it is, you must admit that it has been a motive for murder from time immemorial."

"Oh, I admit it all right. But what about you, Jeffrey?"

The American was silent for a moment. Suddenly he gave a short reckless laugh and Charles saw pain in his eyes. "You're pretty smart, aren't you, Bryce! Okay, I'll tell you how I come to be here. You'll probably find it an amusing story—a real slab of honky-tonk that you've seen in the movies or read in a hundred books. But it wasn't cheap and phoney at the time, sweating it out up there on the Islands. It was heartbreakingly real—and it still is to me."

"You fell in love with this female during the war? Why ever didn't I think of that! The wartime touch is just the last thing needed to complete the trite picture—a backcloth of bombs and blackout."

"Shut up, Ellis! Please go on, Jeffrey."

"Yes, I fell in love with an Aussie girl like so many of our chaps did. I wanted to marry her, but she wanted to wait until the war finished. She said she had to be sure—she did not want to be tied down until things were more settled. She was a Sydney girl, working as a typist with some public relations outfit. She used to tell me about her job and the chap she was working for, a man called—Athol Sefton." He paused before going on. "Well, the time came when we were sent away from Sydney and up to the Islands.

I didn't know when I'd see Barbie again, but she promised she'd wait. She said not to worry about her going around with other chaps, because her job didn't give her much time anyway. That was all right, but on the transport going north I happened to overhear her boss being discussed. Some of our officers had been entertained by Sefton in Sydney and the way they talked about him made me a bit uneasy about Barbie. I kept thinking about a pretty kid like her being in close contact with such a wolf, and had made up my mind to write asking her to take another job when I had a letter from her brother." Jeffrey paused again, tossed off his drink and went to refill his glass.

"Jeffrey, I'm sorry," said Charles quietly. "I saw that letter. I was snooping through the bedrooms and came across it."

The American looked across at him impersonally. "Then you know what happened. Bryce's guess was right in part. What he doesn't know is that I was blamed for Barbie's death. I never told the brother of what I suspected—that Athol Sefton was to blame. I kept quiet on purpose because almost at once I made up my mind to kill Sefton. Someday, somehow, I was going to make him pay for what he had done to Barbie and me. I didn't care how long it took. Time wasn't going to lessen my hate. Even now, when he's dead, I still loathe him as much as I did all those years ago.

"After the war I was sent straight back to the States. I saved until I knew I had enough money for my purpose. First of all I had to find proof of Sefton's guilt. For that I got in touch with a private detective agency in Sydney who managed to find out a few damning details to write me in America. Then I flew over here and got them to trace Sefton's whereabouts and future movements. I got a final report from their Melbourne representative. Sefton was going duck-shooting at a place called Dunbavin. The set-up seemed almost too good to be true. I even had a chance to get a look at this man I had sworn to kill for years. I saw you too," he added to Charles, "at that store where you were buying guns. The agent told me to go there. I think he was hinting I might see Sefton there."

"So it was you who left that note for Athol! And those phone calls in Sydney and the other messages—were they your doing?"

Jeffrey shook his head, puzzled. "I don't know what you're talking about."

"You're quite certain of that? But you did come here to kill Athol."

The American paced up and down the room jerkily. There was a film of perspiration on his face. He looked from Charles to Ellis and back again. "Yes, that's what the Luger was for," he said quietly, "but I didn't get a chance to use it. Someone must have hated Sefton as much as I did and got in first."

"What a sense of anti-climax you must have felt!" said Ellis smoothly. "All that hate which you had been carefully nursing for years gone to waste—not to mention the elaborate plans and ensuing expenditure."

"You mean you don't believe me?"

"Let's say I don't disbelieve you. But I would be singularly guileless if I fell completely for your sob story. Have I the phraseology correct?"

Charles, who had been inclined to believe the American, said hastily, "Quite so. Just because you have confessed to planning to murder Athol does not clear you. While everyone here had an equal opportunity, yours is the strongest motive so far."

"Well, what about Bryce?" asked Jeffrey, an edge to his voice. "Why don't you start snooping in his private affairs? Maybe the reason he's being so helpful is to throw dust in your eyes."

Ellis blinked. "If I committed a murder there would be no need to throw dust, I assure you. But do go on. I can see Charles looking at me with new eyes."

"Okay, I will," said Jeffrey savagely. "You seem to think you're someone set apart from the rest of the world. All that talk last night about being able to spot the killer—you meant yourself! It's just the sort of gag you'd pull and then sit back to think what a smart guy you'd been. I think you gave Jerry back his sweater on purpose this morning and then shot at him yourself."

"Yes, I could have done all that," Ellis agreed meditatively. "But do tell us what you consider was my motive in murdering Athol?"

Jeffrey looked at him contemptuously. "That's easy—jealousy!"

Ellis sat bolt upright. "Jealousy? Now, come, come! I admit I enjoyed a little dalliance once, but—"

"I'm not talking about women. That's not the sort of rivalry you had with Sefton. I mean that the pair of you were alike in so many ways and you couldn't take it. You can't bear not to hold the centre of the stage and neither could he. I thought the first night that you were a pair of conceited wind-bags."

"How very rude of you!" remarked Ellis gently, but there was a note in his voice that caused Charles to glance at him sharply. "If rivalry was the case, then I consider it far more likely that Athol would have attempted to murder me. However, if Charles likes to adopt your motive I'll be happy to sacrifice my self-esteem—if only to be amused by his ever-growing confusion."

"Perhaps I am confused," Charles retorted, "but Jeffrey's suggestion is both feasible and interesting."

"Then you must tell your friend Mr McGrath about it. I'm sure he'd be delighted to advise you."

"Now, what does he mean by that crack?" asked the American, but Charles was spared the necessity of replying by the tempestuous entrance of Jerry Bryce.

"I was looking for you, Carmichael! What the hell do you mean by telling everyone I shot Athol?"

XIV

Charles backed away from Jerry's fiery gaze, bumping into Wilson who had edged aimlessly into the room. "I don't know what the hell you are talking about," he retorted testily.

"Do try and be explicit, my son," Ellis exhorted. "Charles is in a sad state of chaos already."

Jerry continued his menacing advance. "That chap McGrath said you said that I said I shot Athol."

"Wonderful!" applauded Ellis. "As succinct a summary as you could wish for."

"Well, so you did say—I mean, you confessed right at the start, before I even mentioned the possibility of Athol having been murdered."

"That was only because I thought you were accusing Margot."

"I realised that at the time and told you you were making an unnecessary fool of yourself. But now I'm not so sure. People have made ridiculous confessions before this in order to avert suspicion."

"Oh, Charles!" murmured Ellis sadly.

Jerry, thrown off stride, turned on him. "What do you mean— 'Oh, Charles'? Are you going to sit back and let this fellow bleat to every stranger that I'm a killer?"

"Don't vent your tantrum on me," begged his father. "Nothing tires me more. Keep aiming at Charles."

"You'd be far better off if you stuck to your crazy confession," Jeffrey put in. "Carmichael's out to make trouble again, and the more of us who are likely to have murdered Sefton, the safer we are. He can't have the lot of us arrested."

"There are motives converging on poor Charles from all quarters," nodded Ellis. "He doesn't know whom to suspect most. As Mr Jeffrey suggests, we are covered by a sort of insurance as long as we maintain the same rating of motive."

"Your sudden community spirit intrigues me, Ellis," said Charles grimly.

"I can barely recognise myself," the other agreed, "which reminds me—we must do something about Mr Wilson here. I am sure he is too low down on the list for his own safety. Tell me, Mr Wilson, did you have a nice strong motive for murdering Athol Sefton?"

The little field inspector gave a weak smile, as though uncertain of the propriety of a particular parlour game, and shook his head.

"No?" exclaimed Ellis in shocked tones. "Then we must find you one. Let me see now. Neither my motive nor Mr Jeffery's would suit you, I hardly think. What do you suggest, Charles?"

"I suggest you leave Wilson alone," said Charles angrily.

"With your speculative eye on him? Credit me with more feeling for my less fortunate fellow man."

"Didn't Athol once lose you a job or something?" Jerry asked Wilson dispassionately.

"My son!" exclaimed Ellis in fond wonderment. "There is hope for you yet. And after all these years in which I have regarded you as one of those regrettable accidents which befall a man of genius!"

"You'd better not go," advised Jerry, as Wilson, with a sickly smile on his face, moved towards the door. "My father can make up the most ingenious stories. He just can't help himself. In fact, I gave up being ashamed of him years ago."

"A filial blow for a paternal strike! I'll allow it to you, Jerry, to mark this occasion of your sudden evidence of intelligence. Tell us more about Athol's spite against Mr Wilson."

"Actually it was Margot who mentioned it. Wilson was telling her his life's story."

"Why don't you let him speak for himself?" demanded Charles. "Well, Wilson? Is it true that you had some sort of grudge against my uncle?"

The little field inspector, who had been staring unhappily at the floor, looked up. His eyes moved around the circle in a hunted expression and his tongue came out to moisten his lips. He nodded and seemed about to burst into tears. "My wife was sick—dying. I had a p-p-part-time job in a hotel as a drink w-w-"

"Waiter," supplied Ellis wearily, "and you spilled a particularly sticky liqueur all over Athol."

Wilson shook his head violently as though protesting against such a heinous accusation. He made a supreme effort to control his impediment. "I wanted extra m-m-money for my wife. The pay wasn't much, but I thought the tips would be. I used to serve Sefton night after night—big and rich and always with a woman—but he never left anything on the tray. One night I said something to him— my wife had been in great pain that day—told him how much I needed money. But he said that it wasn't anything to do with him and that he never tipped on principle. Then he turned to the blonde tart beside him and winked.

"I was overwrought, thinking of my wife and myself and then of those two so uncaring and well-fed. If he hadn't winked like that—I lifted the tray up and banged it down on his head."

"By jove, I remember the incident now!" said Charles. "It was in one of the Sydney dailies—the only one Athol couldn't stop from publishing the story. It made him look such a fool. They called you the Grand Slammer."

Wilson nodded again. "The name followed me around. People pulled my leg about it. I didn't feel like laughing at the time. You see, my wife died a few days later." He turned aside abruptly, as the emotion overcame him. In the awkward silence which followed, Jerry poured out a drink and pushed it into his hand.

Wilson gulped at it with an averted face, then blew his nose. "Sorry to m-m-make a f-f-" he began, his stammer back.

"Fool of yourself," finished Ellis. "Not at all. A most affecting story—even better than Mr Jeffery's. I like the subtle psychology of it. Though Athol—the unfeeling fellow—was not responsible for Mrs Wilson's death, he is, in Wilson's mind, irrevocably bound up with her sufferings. Well, Charles—I think that accounts for every-one's motive. The Dougalls you dealt with early in the piece—Athol lost them money, the unprincipled cad! Both Adelaide and Margot may be herded into the *crime passionnel* group."

Charles ignored him and addressed Wilson. "You came into your present job with the idea of—ah—renewing acquaintance with Athol?"

"No, it was a coincidence," Jerry interposed, "or so he told Margot. He had no idea he would meet Athol until he saw his name on Aunt Grace's guest list."

"Grace!" exclaimed Ellis. "Charles, what about my sister?"

"Thank you, Ellis, but I'm more interested in Mr Wilson at the moment."

"My dear fellow, what's holding your interest now we know he could also have murdered Athol? Do let us concentrate on Grace. Somebody must fetch her at once. It doesn't matter if the lunch is spoiled."

"I'll go," offered Wilson, making good his escape.

"Damn you, Ellis!" said Charles furiously. "Will you stop making a fool of me!"

"I refuse to reply with the inevitable commonplace."

"The inference your clowning leads me to draw is also inevitable. You are trying to stop my dwelling on your motive."

"I'm with you there, pal," Jeffrey put in.

"Oh, have you found a motive for my father?" asked Jerry, with dispassionate interest. "I wouldn't put it past him to have murdered Athol, but let me tell you that unless he wants you to know, you'll never find out definitely."

"Your quaint proclamation of loyalty moves me, Jerry. And here is Grace! Let's see if she can uphold the Bryce motto of Keeping Them Guessing."

Miss Bryce had an oven cloth in her hand and a harassed expression on her face. "Ellis, what is all this nonsense? That little man told me—you know I haven't time to be—what did you want to see me about?"

"Father says we all had an equal motive and opportunity to

kill Athol Sefton," explained Jerry. "He's not being as crazy as he usually is. He wants to find out if you wanted to murder Athol so that you will be safe."

"No, Grace, don't protest in horror," said Ellis quickly, raising his voice to smother her shocked indrawn breath. "You know perfectly well that you couldn't bear Athol—so rude and always making trouble and how you wished he wouldn't come to the Duck and Dog were some of your very words, my dear."

"I don't deny them," she returned tartly, "but how does—"

"And you were worried about Jerry behaving rashly with him or Shelagh falling in love—"

"My worry is that she never falls in love, though what that has to do—"

"We'll fix a better motive up for Shelagh presently. I feel sure that if Shelagh considered Athol should be murdered, then she would do so efficiently and competently."

"That's a shocking thing for a father to say about his own daughter," said Miss Bryce indignantly. "Whatever are you—"

"Don't get rattled, Aunt," advised Jerry. "It's far better if Charles thinks Shelagh was capable of it."

Charles groaned and dropped his head into his hands. Miss Bryce suddenly rounded on him. "This is all your fault. You shouldn't have started this dreadful story about Mr Sefton being murdered. Like uncle—like nephew—always making trouble!"

"Splendid!" applauded Ellis. "You couldn't have given a worse impression, my dear. Might I add to the record, Charles, that although Grace occasionally pretends to be womanly about firearms, she is no mean shot. Also—"

Charles started up. "I don't want to hear any more," he shouted. "I'm sick and tired of the whole business and the whole lot of you. As far as I'm concerned you can all go and jump into Teal Lagoon. But I'm still going to find out who killed Athol!"

PART THREE

The Impossible Remainder

I

Although she had, early in her marriage with Dr Spenser, reluctantly resigned herself to life in a small country town, Mrs Spenser had resolved never to let herself go. This ambiguous phrase covered not only things like good foundation garments and never being caught in an apron by callers, but also the intellectual side of life.

In Dunbavin her social stocks were high and, being a worthy and energetic citizen, she had built up a continuous round of activity to prevent others from letting themselves go. There was the Reading Circle, the Arts and Crafts Group, the Dunbavin Dramatic Society and the Choral Club. Mrs Spenser was either the president or the chief patroness of them all, but the one nearest her heart was the Reading Circle.

The programme of the Reading Circle consisted of discussion of the latest books and talks by the members on subjects like 'My favourite novel and why' or 'The influence of the Gold Rush on Australian literature'. Occasionally a guest speaker was invited to add to the literary feast, but this was rare and the only Dunbavinites interested in books or lecturing on abstruse subjects were already in the Circle. For this reason, Mrs Spenser always looked forward to the duck season, regarding it as a source of possible speakers.

Surveying the programme she had arranged with the help of the Duck and Dog guests, she felt pleased with the variety it offered. The *pièce de résistance,* she considered, was Charles Carmichael. It was not so much what he was going to lecture on, but what he represented that Mrs Spenser regarded as her own personal triumph.

Every member of the Circle was a subscriber to *Culture and Critic*—in fact, but for the magazine their own culture would have been in a critical way. To the Dunbavin audience that afternoon, Charles was going to be a figurehead of the world of letters.

Dr Spenser came in as his wife was making last-minute adjustments to the circle of chairs in the living room. "Ah, the great day! I trust it will be a successful one, my dear. I must try to look in after surgery."

"Yes, do! You know they all love to see you. And I'm rather relying on you to entertain Ellis Bryce's crowd."

A slow frown settled on the doctor's face. "Oh, they're coming, are they? Will that young fellow, Carmichael, be among them?"

"Yes, and he is going to give a talk," said Mrs Spenser happily.

"I rather wish you hadn't asked him. He was damned impertinent to me, you know, and from what I've been told he's been making a confounded nuisance of himself out at the Dog. I don't want him using your meeting as a platform to air his outlandish notions."

"Oh, I'm sure he won't do that," she replied, without querying what he meant by outlandish notions. "By the way, who was that man who brought Jerry Bryce to the surgery this morning?"

"Fellow by the name of McGrath. Young Jerry did not seem to know much about him. It seems he tagged himself on to Carmichael when he knew there was a room vacant at Bryce's. Why do you ask?"

Mrs Spenser backed up a step or two to regard the effect of a bowl of dahlias. "I was just wondering. Ethel Motherwell told me this McGrath fellow came to see Tom this morning. He was with him for the best part of an hour. Tom seemed rather upset when he'd gone, but he wouldn't tell his mother anything. Rather strange, don't you think?"

"Strange that Sergeant Motherwell managed to hold his tongue for once, or that Mrs Motherwell failed to elicit any information?"

She gave an uncertain smile. "What I meant was why should this stranger McGrath who is staying at the Bryce's want to visit the police?"

"I haven't a notion," returned the doctor shortly, turning to go. But before he left the room he said, "If young Carmichael starts anything, send for me and I'll come and put a stop to it."

Charles, however, had been wishing fervently that he had not allowed himself to be inveigled to the Spensers. "I know these would-be intellectual groups," he remarked gloomily to Shelagh as he helped to clear the tables after lunch. Anyone who wanted to talk to Shelagh was always given some task to perform at the same time. "A bunch of gregarious gas-bags who would be far happier discussing each other's operations than literature."

"They do that at the Social Committee meeting," replied Shelagh, with a smile. "The Reading Circle is an earnest affair."

"That makes it worse. Earnest people are a blight on the community."

"I rather admire the characteristic."

"Then I must try to cultivate it. I would like you to approve of something about me." He gave her a sidelong glance to gauge the effect of his words, but she went on stacking plates without a change of expression. He tried another gambit as he took one end of the table-cloth she held out silently. "Shelagh, if I told you I was tired, depressed and feel as though I haven't a friend in the world, what would you say?"

"I'd say you were run-down and need a course of vitamin injections," she answered briskly.

"Don't be clinical," he implored, allowing the cloth to be twitched from his fingers and holding his hands at the ready for another to be tossed to him. "My mental shape calls for a more psychological treatment."

"You mean womanly sympathy, I suppose. What a pity Mrs Turner has left. She seemed good at that kind of thing."

He brightened. "I liked the way you said that. There was a faintly jealous note."

"Don't flatter yourself," she said coldly. "And please hurry up with the table-cloth. I've got a lot to do before I go out."

"Where are you going?"

"To Mrs Spenser's—with you. Someone has to see to it that you behave yourself."

"You certainly have a lowering effect on a man," he said doubtfully. "Athol told me you were the hardest nut he ever tried to crack. He called you his brilliant failure."

"Athol—" she began, and then abruptly changed her tone and subject. "Charles, what are you and McGrath going to do? Jerry was telling me about the scene this morning."

"That was your respected parent's doing. He had everyone owning up to a motive for murdering Athol—even your Aunt Grace. Oh, a very humorous man, your father—so puckish!"

"Yes, he can be annoying. Jerry said he left McGrath in Dunbavin."

"He told me he had some commissions to perform. You know, of course, that he thinks or pretends to think that I murdered both my aunt and Athol—a belief that has been strengthened by his discovery of the missing Wilding rifle under the seat of my car. He intends sending it down to town for a ballistics check."

The girl looked at him with an anxious frown. "That puts you in rather a bad position, doesn't it? What are you going to do?"

He threw out his hands in a helpless gesture that, had he but known, made more impression on her than anything he had done or said before. "I just haven't a clue."

II

Mrs Spenser advanced with gracious outstretched hands as her guests from the Duck and Dog entered the living room. "How charming of you all to come! Some of your big family are already at home, Ellis." She indicated the Turners sitting somewhat subdued in a corner and McGrath wedged in a group of Dunbavin intellectuals. "You didn't tell me you had a police inspector staying with you. He has been entertaining us with some of his experiences. Quite fascinating!"

"How remiss of me!" said Ellis smoothly. "I really guessed something of the kind, you know, Charles."

Mrs Spenser transferred her clinging hand. "Welcome to our little group, Mr Carmichael. We are looking forward so much to your talk. Such a stimulating and provocative subject, the—ah—*roman policier*! My dear Mrs Dougall!"

Mrs Dougall extended a hand like a Headquarters C.O.'s wife visiting a hill station. "Did I understand you to say that man is a detective?"

"Why, yes. Didn't you know?"

"Jumbo, did you hear that? One certainly rubs shoulders with the strangest people nowadays. Adelaide, have you those albums? Just a few photographs I have brought along to pass around as I give my lecture."

"Well, come along everybody, and we'll get down to work," cried Mrs Spenser, clapping her hands.

"The identity of your friend has shaken us all," Ellis murmured in Charles's ear, as their hostess moved on to greet the others. "Tell me—is it going to be like one of those books you review? After amassing a weight of evidence quite unknown to the hapless reader, the great detective stands up at a most fortuitous gathering of the suspects and points the accusing finger. The guilty one, like a good sportsman, acknowledges his guilt by either swallowing the cyanide tablet hidden in his signet ring or by blowing his brains out with his pistol disguised as a pipe."

"How I'd like that finger to be pointed at you!" rejoined Charles, dividing his scowl equally between Ellis and McGrath, who raised a laconic hand at him in greeting.

Ellis slapped his pockets. "No gun, and I left off carrying cyanide after my first successful murder. Of course, there is always the crashing leap through the window, but what hope has one of breaking one's neck amongst Mrs Spenser's flowers? It shall have to be an attempted getaway, foiled by the stalwart arms of Tom Motherwell who has been warned of the possibility and is stationed outside."

He broke off and gave a sound of mild surprise. "Well, well! I never thought the devil would appear in the guise of our worthy sergeant."

A hush fell over the room as Sergeant Motherwell came in, tightly uniformed and looking self-conscious with a certain air of importance. After a word to Mrs Spenser, he crossed to where McGrath was sitting and handed him a folded piece of paper. McGrath glanced at it casually, smiled affably at the ring of curious faces about him, then put it in his pocket.

Quelling an impulse to rush over and enquire what was going on, Charles strolled to the back of the room where Margot Stainsbury had signalled to him. Mrs Spenser had taken up her position at the opposite end, flashed a presidential smile around the gathering and announced the meeting of the Dunbavin Reading Circle open.

"Charles," said Margot carefully. "What have we got ourselves into? How has it all come about? I've got the craziest feeling it must be a dream."

"More like a dashed nightmare. Just another thing we've got Athol to thank for."

"Athol—Chas, you're not going to do anything silly here, are you? You and that McGrath person?"

He pretended not to hear as he watched Mrs Dougall being guided to the speaker's table amid clapping led loudly by Major

Dougall. Under cover of the applause, McGrath leaned back in his chair and spoke to Shelagh who was sitting beside him. Soon Mrs Dougall was booming away about hot Indian nights and the sounds of the jungle and passing out slightly dimmed and dog-eared photographs. Charles found Shelagh handing him a picture of a slimmer Major Dougall standing triumphantly beside a supine carcass.

"McGrath said to tell you the bullet matched Father's Wilding," the girl whispered. "Tom Motherwell just brought word."

"Ah—so he agrees now that Athol was murdered! It's a pity he didn't take my word for it in the first place."

She made no rejoinder, apparently intent on Mrs Dougall's discourse. Presently, giving a sidelong glance, Charles caught her troubled gaze fixed on him.

"What is the matter? What else did McGrath say?"

"He said that you still topped his suspect list. Charles, what are you going to do? He can't really mean that."

"Oh yes he can," he muttered back grimly, only partly comforted by her concern.

Mrs Dougall came to the end of her tiger hunt and waited for the applause, displaying both rows of her dentures which looked like trophies of the same shoot. Still clapping, Mrs Spenser came to stand beside her and presently raised her hands for silence. "Well, I'm sure we all enjoyed that most interesting talk. And now for something in a lighter vein from Mrs Andrew Turner. I understand this will take the form of—what was it again, Mrs Turner?"

Frances gave a shy murmur and shrank back in her corner. Her husband nudged her sharply. "It's a kind of sketch. She takes people off," he announced. "Go on, Frankie!"

Momentarily diverted from his predicament, Charles braced himself to listen to a few shoddy imitations of well-known film stars. Frances stood in front of the table, staring about the room as though stricken with stage-fright. Then quite calmly she moved the table to one side, flicking at it with an invisible duster and talking about her actions in complaining half-sentences.

Shelagh stirred and murmured in a quivering voice, "Good heavens! It's Aunt Grace! She even looks like her." Almost at once a ripple of amusement went through the audience. As the impersonation was recognised, Frances slipped into another. She seemed to grow taller and carried her head at a quizzical tilt. The bored, half-supercilious tones were uncanny in their likeness to Ellis Bryce. From the back of the room, Jerry let out an unfilial guffaw which ricocheted back as the girl started slouching about with hands in invisible pockets and denouncing the world.

"We'd better not laugh too soon," said Charles. "I've a notion we're all in for a rubbing." He turned round to find out who was breathing so heavily on the back of his neck and discovered Sergeant Motherwell watching him. Realising by whose orders he was standing guardian, Charles shot a fulminating glance at McGrath who grinned amiably back at him.

"Darling, we're being butchered to make a Dunbavin holiday," Margot drifted up to murmur plaintively. "Let's all fume together."

Loud applause greeted the end of the clever performance. Frances hung her head as Mrs Spenser, who regarded herself as a soul of tact, made a little speech of thanks endeavouring at the same time to smooth down any possible ruffled feathers.

"I have persuaded Mrs Turner to show us what she can really do. She has undertaken to recite a little poem which I am sure will be more in keeping with our little gathering here." A suitable gravity replaced the audience's rollicking mood at this reproof. Shyly and hesitantly, as though she were in disgrace, Frances began to recite.

"Do you know what it's all about?" asked a voice presently in Charles's ear, leaving a mingled smell of antiseptic and halitosis. Dr Spenser had entered the room with elaborate caution. Seeing Charles, he had come to stand alongside with the intention of dealing firmly with an outburst.

"'—famished, splintered, white, wrenched from its life, yet dying with grace—'" Frances finished her poem, then scuttled to Andrew's side.

"These literary affairs are rather beyond me," declared the doctor humorously, to show that he was not afraid to admit ignorance. "My wife is, of course, quite in her element. Here she comes now! My dear, I was asking Mr Carmichael to explain the significance of the verses we have just heard."

She slapped his hand playfully. "How like you to pretend! They were called 'The Broken Bough'—lovely, lovely words! What are you hovering around for, Tom Motherwell? I declare I don't know what's got into everyone this afternoon. Will you come up to the table now, Mr Carmichael? It's your turn."

Rather red around the neck, Sergeant Motherwell retreated. He sat down beside McGrath, and after a whispered consultation which everyone strained to hear, both policemen folded their arms and waited for Charles to begin his talk on The Detective Novel.

Thoroughly versed in his subject, though feeling strangely little of his customary enthusiasm for it, he began with the birth of detective fiction under the authorships of Poe, Conan Doyle and Wilkie Collins, declaring it to be a literary form of high distinction. He sounded so authoritative and easy as he traced the development of the genre down through the years, naming a few classic titles, listing some of the abuses to which it had been subjected and enumerating its tenets, that the members of the Dunbavin Reading Circle sat up ready to be intelligent at question time. Mrs Spenser was immensely pleased with him and forgot her curiosity as to the tension the guests from the Duck and Dog had brought into her living room. She made an enthusiastic speech of thanks at the conclusion of Charles's lecture and then announced coyly that tea and stronger refreshments would be served.

Charles moved thankfully to a quiet corner. Almost at once McGrath appeared beside him. "Hullo, boy?" he greeted him imperturbably. "Have a cup of tea. You've earned it after all that gab."

"All right, Mac! What's the score? I gather you haven't come to talk about my lecture—not after having set that fool Motherwell on to me all this afternoon."

McGrath took a noisy sip of tea, set his cup in its saucer and took an outsize bite from a small-sized scone. "You wouldn't want me to make a scene in this high-brow atmosphere, would you? However, you might as well know now as later that I'm getting a warrant issued for your arrest."

"Oh, now, look here!" said Charles wearily. "A joke's a joke, but—"

"No joke, boy! I know you've been going flat out trying to pin your uncle's murder on the good people, here, but—"

"Good people be damned! Any one of them could have murdered Athol. What about Wilson? And Jeffrey has admitted planning to kill him."

McGrath shrugged. "We'll wait until after the party. You'd better enjoy what's left of it." With these ominous words he moved away.

"Charles!"

He turned to find Shelagh standing behind him, and tried to smile. "I've been behaving myself, haven't I?"

A sparkle of something like anger shone in her eyes. "I heard what McGrath said. We must do something quickly. It's—it's absurd that you're in this position." She drew him further away and spoke in an urgent undertone. "I've got an idea. It might sound crazy, but something you said in your lecture made me think of it."

"What was that? I can't remember a thing I said—what with Mac watching my every move and Motherwell ready to clap a heavy hand on my shoulder."

"The process of eliminating the impossible suspects of a murder, so that whatever remains is the answer, however improbable."

He gazed about the room at the various guests from the Duck and Dog and said bitterly, "I've already tried to make that rule apply. But in this case there's a positive phalanx of probable suspects. Take them away and the answer is impossible."

She did not speak for a moment; then she said quietly, "Perhaps that is the answer. What could be more impossible than someone called Morton who booked at the Duck and Dog for the duck season and then did not arrive?"

Slowly and incredulously, Charles turned his head. For a long moment he stared at her, the blank look in his eyes gradually becoming enlivened and alert. "Shelagh! You wonderful girl!" he breathed.

"The booking was made through the Happy Holiday Agency," said Shelagh. "Then a telegram arrived signed Morton, cancelling it at the last moment."

There was another long pause as Charles wrestled with a hundred stabbing thoughts, while her expressive eyes encouraged him. He glanced around the room again. "I've got to get out of here," he decided swiftly, "without Mac catching me. Can you keep him occupied in some way? He's over in the corner with Dr Spenser."

"I'll try."

He watched her move slowly across the room as he edged around the outskirts of the crowd. Her usually brisk gait seemed faltering and uncertain. She spoke a few words to Dr Spenser, put one hand up to cover her eyes, then quietly sagged against McGrath.

In an instant the room was in confusion and Charles, grinning in admiration at the best interpretation he had ever seen of the oldest trick in the world, slipped quietly out.

III

Lights were beginning to wink when Charles reached the outer suburbs of Melbourne, and the haze over the city was shot with mauve from advertising signs. With an anxious glance at his wrist-watch, he pulled up at a public telephone booth, thumbed hastily through the dog-eared directory and, dialling a number, prayed for luck to favour him. At the lifting of the receiver he sent his coppers rolling. "I want to speak to either Mr Dawson or Mr Stanley."

"This is Stanley speaking."

"My name is Carmichael. A client of yours—Mr Harris Jeffrey—gave me your name. I've come down from the country to see you on a matter of great importance."

"You are fortunate to have caught me, Mr Carmichael. It's well after consulting hours."

"Well, put in some overtime. I'll be there within half an hour." Charles replaced the receiver, rubbed his hands gleefully and went back to his car.

Twenty-five minutes later he was on the fourth floor of a block of offices in the heart of the city, knocking on the frosted glass panel which bore the words DAWSON AND STANLEY—PRIVATE ENQUIRY SPECIALISTS—AFFILIATIONS IN ALL STATES AND OVERSEAS.

"Are you Stanley?" he asked the discreet-looking little man who answered. "I rang a little while ago. Thank you for waiting."

"Come into the inner office, Mr Carmichael. Am I right in presuming you are the late Athol Sefton's nephew?"

Charles followed him into a quiet, comfortably furnished room. "How did you know I was related to Athol Sefton?"

The little man tutted in self-reproach. "A regrettable lapse in discretion. But he has been in my mind continually since I saw in the papers that he had met with a fatal shooting accident. Please accept my condolences."

"Oh—er—thanks very much. As a matter of fact it is connected with my uncle's death that I want to consult you. You see, it is my belief—now somewhat belatedly shared by the police—that Athol was not accidentally shot, but deliberately and cleverly murdered."

"Dear me, what a shocking thing!" exclaimed Stanley. "A dreadful thing! And you say Mr Jeffrey sent you to us? Is he in some kind of—ah—trouble?"

"He could be. He is one of a group of people at the Duck and Dog hotel near Dunbavin where I was staying with my uncle; each one of them had an excellent motive for murdering him."

The agent blinked at him nervously. "We have severed our connection with Mr Jeffrey. And I assure you in a case of murder—"

"I didn't come here on Jeffrey's behalf," Charles assured him. "But on my own. I want some information and I think you might be able to help me."

Stanley regarded him warily. "What sort of information, Mr Carmichael?"

Charles leaned across the desk. "Mr Jeffrey employed you to trace my uncle's movements up to the time he went to the Duck and Dog. Is it possible that you might have been spying on Athol for yet another person's benefit? Someone other than Jeffrey knew that my uncle would probably purchase a gun for duck-shooting at a certain place in the city."

The agent raised a pained hand. "Not spying, I beg of you. We are a reputable organisation. Yes, there have been occasions prior to Mr Jeffrey's instructions when we have been asked to enquire into your late uncle's affairs."

"What were those occasions?"

"Let me see now." Stanley rose and went to a filing cabinet in a corner of the room. Presently he drew out a folder and turned over its contents. "There was an investigation job we did for a finance group Sefton was trying to interest in some project, but that was quite some years ago. Oh—and here are two divorce cases we worked on."

"I know about them," said Charles impatiently. "I want information a bit more up-to-date. Those divorces were over and done with before his wife died."

"His wife? Now that would be your Aunt Paula, would it not? Would you be interested in knowing we were once asked to do a little job on Mrs Sefton?"

"When was this?" asked Charles quickly, wondering why the agent was regarding him so coyly.

"About a year ago. Our Sydney associates wrote asking for information about a certain party for a client of theirs who wanted a full report on Mrs Sefton. I have their letter here."

"Who was the certain party?"

Stanley coughed and looked away. "You might recall that I knew who you were when you stepped into this office."

"You mean I was the party you investigated?"

"I assure you there was nothing of a derogatory nature in the report we sent back to our associates. Your character and mode of living seemed quite blameless and your relations with your aunt of the most amiable. In fact, 'devoted' was the word I used while describing such little attentions as your habit of sending chocolates to Mrs Sefton."

Charles jumped from his chair. "You say you told your Sydney client I sent Aunt Paula chocolates? Quickly—what was the name of the client?"

"I'm afraid I can't tell you, but I daresay I can find out. I'll ring our Sydney office first thing in the morning. At the same time, I can enquire if there was anyone else interested in Athol Sefton's duck-shooting expedition to Dunbavin. How will that suit you?"

Charles curbed his impatience. "I'll call you early in the morning. Thanks for your help."

Stanley accompanied him to the door. "You haven't told me, Mr Carmichael, just why you want this information. Surely the police—"

"The police should be doing this work, you mean? I couldn't agree with you more, but it so happens that they consider I shot Athol and poisoned my aunt as well."

IV

After calling at an interstate airline terminal to book a seat on the morning plane to Sydney, Charles drove out of the city toward his bachelor flat. Once Dawson and Stanley provided the necessary information he intended to call on their mysterious Sydney client.

A mouth-drooling smell of frying bacon wafted to greet him as he let himself into his flat. He paused, sniffed it happily, then frowned and banged the doors shut.

"Is that you, boy?" called a voice, as he strode through the living room to the kitchen. "How do you like your eggs?"

"What the hell are you doing here?"

McGrath, a tea-towel pinned around his waist, waved an egg at him then broke it over the frying pan with a flourish. "Cooking our supper. That porter of yours is an amiable bloke. He let me have some bread and a bottle of milk. The rest of the stuff I found in the 'fridge."

"Oh, so it was Judd who let you in. Did you tell him you were a policeman?"

"No, just an old pal. Sit down, boy, and ease that mean look off your face."

"I don't take kindly to this intrusion, Mac. If you are looking for the coffee, try the cannister marked 'coffee'. It is rather unusual for you to deviate from the obvious."

"Funny thing, but my wife keeps anything *but* what is labelled in these tins. That's women for you. They never act according to the rules."

Charles began to slice bread to put in the toaster. "So we're going to discuss women, are we?"

"Just a passing comment. Here, wrap your stomach round this."

Charles surveyed the proffered plate and suddenly laughed. "Do you usually serve bacon and eggs before making an arrest?"

"Only to my pets," returned McGrath equably, taking his place at the table. "Talking of women and the way they disregard the generally accepted, Miss Bryce certainly caused you to break out in a rash."

"The woman's touch was evidently what I needed," said Charles, getting up to take the percolator off the fire. "Pass your cup over."

"Thanks. While you're up, get some more butter, will you?"

"Go easy or there won't be any left over for breakfast. I take it you will be here for breakfast?" added Charles sardonically.

"I'll be here," agreed McGrath cheerfully, "but don't let me disturb you. I've slept on worse beds than that couch of yours in the living room."

"Allow me to offer my bed. I'll take the couch."

"Very good of you, I'm sure, but I wouldn't consider accepting such a sacrifice."

"You mean you want to be between me and the exits," said Charles dryly.

"There might be something in what you say too," nodded the detective affably.

"Mac, you've got to give me a chance. I've got the craziest notion that I'm on the right track at last over this business."

McGrath heaved himself up to pour more coffee. "I'm giving you more chances than I ever gave anyone before, boy. You won't mind if I hang around while you play your games? I've got my own neck to think of, you know."

"You stay around and I'll present the murderer to you on a platter," Charles promised.

They finished their meal together amiably and cleared up. Then Charles found blankets for his guest, and went off to shave and bathe. On his way back from the bathroom, he put his head into the living room and spoke the thought that had come to him under the shower. "George Washington slept here! Athol used that couch just before we went to Dunbavin."

"He did? Wouldn't he take your offer either?"

"No, he seemed to want to keep me under his eye as much as you do now. I trust you don't intend popping in and out to see if I'm asleep?"

"Sefton did that, did he? Well, you couldn't blame him for being jumpy, could you?"

"I know what inference I should draw from that, but I've got my own ideas."

"They'd better be good," declared McGrath on a mighty yawn. "Good-night, boy! Don't use the drain-pipe outside your window like a good chap."

"It would be beneath my dignity. Good-night, Towser—and don't bark at every noise."

At breakfast the following morning, Charles said grudgingly, "You may as well know—I've booked a flight to Sydney this morning. I suppose you'll want to tag along."

McGrath looked up placidly from a plate of cereal. "It'll be nice to see the old home town. What would you be wanting to do in Sydney, boy?"

"Never mind! Hurry up, I've got a job to do in Melbourne first."

"What sort of job?"

"You work it out. I can't help your looking over my shoulder all the time, but I'm damned if I'm going to give a word-for-word explanation."

"Okay—keep your shirt on! I thought maybe I could save you some trouble."

"Well, that's a change," remarked Charles acidly.

In the city, he sought out the holiday booking office which handled Ellis Bryce's erratic affairs. "The Duck and Dog Hotel? queried the clerk, when Charles said he wanted some information. "They're pretty well booked up for the moment."

"Yes, I know," said Charles impatiently. "I'm staying there."

The clerk looked bewildered. "What information is it you were wanting then?"

"I want to know the address of some people called Morton who made a reservation through this office and then did not arrive. At the last moment there was a vacant room."

"A vacant room?" repeated the clerk, shocked. "Mr Bryce did not advise us of this."

"Oh, he let some casual tourists have it. Can you get that information immediately? It's very important and I'm in a great hurry."

There was a telephone on the counter nearby and Charles reached for it. "Do you mind if I use your phone?" he added, dialling rapidly.

"You know, boy, you remind me of someone out of the movies," murmured McGrath admiringly.

"Well, that's a change from being likened to someone out of a book," retorted Charles. "I assure you I am not trying to emulate either—Hullo? I want to speak to Mr Stanley, please."

"Would this be of interest to you, sir?" interrupted the clerk, sliding across the counter a letter to which the duplicate of a receipt was clipped. "The booking was made by mail with a deposit enclosed. We sent an endorsement and a receipt back."

"Thanks—is that Mr Stanley? Carmichael speaking. Did you— Oh, nice work! Just a minute—I want to write it down."

"Allow me!" McGrath offered his fountain pen.

"What was it again, Stanley?" Charles held the pen poised on the letter in front of him, ready to jot down notes. "Yes, I remember the case you mentioned—and you say there was someone else after Athol, as I thought? What? The same name and address? That's interesting. Yes—yes—what!"

"Take it easy!" advised McGrath, amused though baffled.

Charles lowered his voice. "Say that again, will you, Stanley— right! And the address? That means your Sydney associate never had any personal contact with the client? Well, thanks very much— you've been a great help. No, I don't think I'll need anything more. Eh?. Oh—er—thanks! Good-bye." Charles put the receiver back and, grinning from ear to ear, said inanely, "He wished me every success."

"Fancy! Now that was nice of him! Is Stanley his Christian or surname?"

"Oh, I forgot you are not as advanced in this case as I am. Dawson and Stanley are the private enquiry agents Harry Jeffrey used to trace Athol."

"Don't be cocky, boy," drawled McGrath.

"I've got every reason to be. The information he provided ties up with this." He picked up the letter lovingly and folded it carefully away into his wallet. "You don't mind, do you?" he asked the bewildered clerk disarmingly.

"Er—no. I suppose not."

"That's fine. Come on, Mac! I want to buy some chocolates before we catch that plane."

V

Three hours later McGrath was trailing Charles around the streets of another city. "Pavements are the same anywhere," the detective complained. "And I thought I'd given up pounding them years ago. Don't your feet hurt?"

"Nope!" replied Charles cheerfully, but he hailed a taxi coming down from King's Cross.

"Where to now?" asked McGrath, loosening the laces of his shoes with an agonised expression.

Charles gave an address to the driver. "We're going to call on the people who booked that room at the Duck and Dog."

"It's to be hoped you find them in after coming all this way."

Charles did not reply. He pulled out a cigarette and smoked rapidly, sitting forward on the seat as the taxi sped along the steep curving streets.

Presently McGrath observed, "Why don't you relax, boy? You're making me nervous."

Charles laughed shortly. "You show the quaintest humour. Okay, driver, this looks like it."

"I can read too, mate," said the man in an injured tone, as he pulled the wheel around. What number was it you wanted?"

"Forty-three. Should be up the other end."

They cruised slowly down a plush-looking residential street, lined with modern mansions set in half-grown landscaped gardens.

"Classy quarter," remarked McGrath on a yawn.

"Yes. You couldn't possibly be suspicious about an address like this, could you?"

The street ended in a small headland overlooking the harbour. The taxi pulled up at the railing erected to check the unwary. "Looks like your number should be just about where the breakers are," was the driver's comment. "Sure you've got it right, mate?"

"Turn around and drive down the other side slowly," Charles ordered, checking the address on the letter. "Street numbers get haywire sometimes."

Shrugging, the man reversed and turned, while Charles craned out the window. "Any luck?" asked McGrath, when they reached the end again.

Charles settled back in his seat once more. "No luck. All right, driver, back to town."

"You don't seem overly disturbed at missing your party, boy."

"No, I'm not," said Charles exuberantly.

"Cracking hardy, or did you perhaps expect it?"

Charles looked at him. "You're quite a bright bird when you take your head out of the sand. The people called Morton who booked at the Duck and Dog never had any intention of turning up, because in simple fact they didn't even exist." When the detective made no comment, he added, "I want to look in at Athol's office now. Perhaps you'd like to see your own people? Could I drop you anywhere?

"You wouldn't be wanting to get rid of me, would you?"

"Now, whatever gave you that idea?"

"Perhaps I was being oversensitive," the other rejoined, equally bland. "Tell me, how does that classy magazine of yours function with its managing editor dead and its sub-editor on the run?"

"It functions very smoothly in the hands of an efficient female, appropriately named Miss Smart. The only woman Athol never tried to undermine."

"I take it she was more necessary to his business life than to his sex life. How did the lady like the arrangement?"

"I never heard her complain. She is one of these career-minded women who are never stumped when it comes to their jobs. I must try and catch her out on something we heard at that ridiculous party of Mrs Spenser's."

The head office of *Culture and Critic* was rather like a hotel suite. Lushly carpeted, discreetly lighted and bearing on its elegant walls blown-up photographs of the great and small in the world of the arts, it drew a soft, rude whistle from McGrath.

"Athol always believed in keeping up appearances," declared Charles with a grin. "Hullo, Miss Smart! Surprise!"

A woman about forty with the appearance of a well-groomed racehorse had emerged from an inner room to answer to the muted chime bell. Her blue-rinsed grey hair clung as smoothly to her skull as the black suit was moulded to her strictly controlled figure. A touch of lace on her blouse and a large sapphire ring on one white but capable hand were her only concessions to charm. She greeted Charles calmly and said the right number of words in the right manner about Athol's death.

Charles introduced McGrath. "Come into Athol's office, Miss Smart. There are a few things I want to talk about. You may be able to help."

"Certainly, Mr Carmichael. I think you'll find everything has been running smoothly here. I have been making a day-to-day report since I heard about Mr Sefton's accident."

"It's not the magazine I want to talk about, but Mr Sefton himself. Mac, for Pete's sake stop gaping and sit down!"

"Sorry, boy. I'm over-awed by the way the other half work."

"Could I fix you gentlemen a drink?" suggested Miss Smart.

The yellow went out of Charles's eye. "An excellent notion. We could both do with one."

When she had trod noiselessly over the deep grey carpet to a cocktail cabinet on the other side of the room, McGrath said in an appreciative undertone, "I must mention this lay-out to the Commissioner at our next Heads of Department conference. He is always calling for suggestions to facilitate smoother organisation."

After she had presented the men with a long tinkling glass apiece, Miss Smart merged herself into the background. The phone on Athol's immense desk rang a couple of times, and after the second call, she told the switch-girl to take messages as there was an important meeting about to commence. Charles took the hint, drained his glass, and said briskly, "I want to know everything you can tell me about Mr Sefton's behaviour prior to his departure from Melbourne. First of all, Miss Smart, did you know he intended going duck-shooting?"

"Not definitely. But as it had been his custom to do so over the past few years, I presumed he had gone to Dunbavin. When I arrived here at the office last Friday there was a note on my desk saying he would be away for a week or so. But there was no mention of where he had gone."

"Then you didn't know that he had booked a flight to Melbourne under an assumed name?"

Miss Smart looked surprised. "No, I didn't. As a rule he asked me to arrange his travelling. But lately there have been sudden lapses from his normal manner."

"Ah!" exclaimed Charles involuntarily. "Have you any idea what caused these lapses?"

Miss Smart turned the sapphire on her finger reflectively. "Not the precise cause, but I remember he seemed particularly upset one day over a letter in his mail. Then there were occasional telephone calls which seemed to arouse the same agitation."

"Do you know who could have been ringing Mr Sefton?"

She shook her head. "Mr Sefton received many calls. The letter too must have been in his private mail."

There was a pause, then Charles asked, "Does the name Morton convey anything to you?"

"I can't recollect anyone of that name being connected with Mr Sefton, not at the moment," she answered slowly. "Perhaps if I had a little time to ponder?"

"I wish you would. We'll go and get a bite of lunch now and come back later. Ready, Mac?" He picked up his hat and, followed by McGrath, crossed the room. At the door he paused. "Oh, by the way, Miss Smart, I've been telling Mr McGrath here that I've never known you to be stumped. Let's show him how good you can be. Will you trace this for me?"

He came back to the desk, thought for a moment, then scrawled a few hesitant words on the memorandum pad. McGrath was looking over his shoulder in a trice. "Oh, poetry!" said the latter in mock disgust. "Is that all!"

VI

Charles hailed a cruising taxi. "Manonetta's".

McGrath's eyebrows surged upwards once more. "We're certainly moving in the best circles."

"Athol always lunched there. You know these calls Miss Smart talked about and the letter?"

"What about them?"

"The person who killed Athol wasn't content to merely murder him. There was a build-up of refined torture in the shape of threatening calls and messages. Margot Stainsbury told me about Athol receiving a phone call when she lunched with him a week or so ago."

"And you're hoping to trace the call?" asked McGrath sadly. "I wish you luck, boy. I've only known that stunt to come off in books."

"Oh, shut up about books!" snapped Charles.

Manonetta's, a restaurant of deep carpets, discreet lighting and huge menus, was filled with lunchers who knew the value of being seen in the right places no matter what the cost. They had to wait some time for the head waiter, who looked like a Renaissance prince, to come to them. Charles slipped a note into an unprincely palm. "My name is Carmichael. My uncle, Mr Athol Sefton, always lunched here."

Head waiters have good memories. "Delighted to see you again, Mr Carmichael. Mr Sefton not with you today?"

"No, but could we have his usual table?"

"Yes, indeed, sir. If you would just follow me?"

He led the way deftly through the crowded room and was about to eject skilfully but gently a pair of brightly chattering females from a centre table when Charles remembered what Margot had said. "No, not here. Last time he had a table in the corner."

"Pardon! You want his unusual table? Just over here, sir."

They were settled tenderly into the chairs and the wine waiter was summoned by a lifted eyebrow. "Before you go," said Charles, "the last time Mr Sefton lunched here, he had a lady with him. A dark, rather striking, lady."

"Ah, that would be Miss Stainsbury—the model? I recollect perfectly."

"Good! Do you also recollect Mr Sefton being called away to take a telephone call?"

The head waiter's alertness became clouded. "I regret I do not remember. Gaetano! You heard the gentleman. Do you recall a telephone call to Mr Athol Sefton?"

The wine waiter looked blank for a moment, then light dawned and he spoke in rapid Italian. His superior listened, then glanced at Charles curiously. "Gaetano remembers."

"He also remembers Mr Sefton was somewhat upset by the call," suggested Charles.

"Signor Carmichael understands Italian?"

"No, but he's still a smart lad," vouchsafed McGrath. "Okay, boy, you've made your point. What about eating now?"

"Order what you like and make it for two," Charles replied absently. His air of abstraction lasted throughout the meal, but did not deter McGrath from enjoying a hearty repast. He declared at the end that if only the Police Department would see its way to providing cost plus expense sheets for its officers, he too would lunch daily at Manonetta's.

"Glad you like it. Come on, if you're still following me. I want to call in at the G. P. O."

McGrath groaned. "You haven't still got the notion of trying to trace a telephone call, have you?"

"I think they usually keep some sort of record of long-distance calls."

"What makes you think it might be a trunk-line call?"

"I'll explain when things begin to tie up more—that is, if you want to listen."

"I'll listen, as long as you don't expect me to believe anything."

"You consider it's a simpler solution to imagine me guilty, don't you?"

"If I were in your place, I would just admit everything for the sake of peace and quiet. These tortuous investigations of yours are wearing both of us down. What about it, boy?" he added coaxingly.

Charles gave him a burning glance, and the detective raised a pacifying hand. "All right, all right! Let's go and trace a phone call."

The telephone people were not at all in favour of Charles's request, and were about to issue a firm but polite refusal when McGrath rose nobly to the occasion and produced his police card. At once, a member of the staff was delegated to the search and, in spite of McGrath's pessimism, a slip of paper headed 'In-Docket' was unearthed in a surprisingly short time. Charles was jubilant and almost embraced the unembraceable-looking female who had produced the evidence.

"Cranbilka!" said McGrath. "That's about two hundred miles south-west from Sydney. Quite a nice little town, I believe."

"How can I find out the name of the person who put this call through from Cranbilka to Mr Sefton at Manonetta's?" Charles asked the telephonist.

"That would be quite an impossible task, I'm afraid. The call was made from a public telephone at the local post-office. The chances are very slight that the telephonist on duty would remember—even if she happened to see the caller, which is doubtful."

Charles thanked her and off they went. "We'll go back to the office now. There are one or two points I want to check—which includes a map—and then I'll start laying some cards on the table."

There was a map of the eastern States attached to a wall in a small store-room off Athol's office, which was marked with various coloured pins to indicate the circulation centres of *Culture and Critic*.

"Now show me this place, Cranbilka," requested Charles, surveying it.

McGrath traced along a highway leading from the city with his forefinger. "Should be about here, I'd say. Yes, here you are—where the yellow pin is."

"Not one of our better customers," was Charles's comment, as he followed the route in his turn. "Aha! That makes Fisherton about the half-way mark."

"What's Fisherton got to do with things? I thought you were interested in Cranbilka."

"I'm keenly interested in both places—as I'll explain in a moment. But first I want to see Miss Smart."

Athol's secretary was seated in her comfortable office dictating into a recorder. She switched it off when the two men entered. "I didn't know you had returned from lunch, Mr Carmichael. I have that information you required."

"You have? Splendid!"

"Regarding the name Morton—there is only one I can put my finger on at the moment. We have a distributing agent of that name at a country town called Cranbilka."

Grinning triumphantly, Charles turned to McGrath and clapped him on the shoulder. "Well, how am I doing, boy? Pretty good?"

"If you say so," said McGrath cautiously.

"Miss Smart, I want you to put a call through to this fellow Morton at Cranbilka. Tell him we're running a sort of survey and would like to know the names and something about his subscribers to *Culture and Critic*. I'll be in Mr Sefton's office."

"Very well, Mr Carmichael," said the secretary imperturbably. "By the way, I managed to locate that quotation you asked about. You'll find the book of verses on Mr Sefton's desk."

"Eh? Oh yes, thanks. There you are, Mac! What did I tell you?"

McGrath followed him back to Athol's office. "Why didn't you ask her to get information about Morton? Isn't he the one you want?"

Charles sat down behind the desk. "I don't think so. It is my belief that Morton, our agent for *Culture and Critic*, has also been the agent—probably unwittingly—for the murderer."

"So you think Sefton was killed by someone from Cranbilka?"

"I am sure of it. That call we traced proves it."

McGrath did not speak. "Well, doesn't it?" asked Charles irritably, picking up the slim volume of verse Miss Smart had left and snapping the covers open and shut. "Athol was being tormented by threatening letters and calls, one of which we know came from Cranbilka."

"Why don't you settle for your pal Morton if that is the case?"

"I tell you Morton doesn't exist in this case except as a name. The murderer had to move anonymously and from an association of ideas adopted the name Morton. That is why I have asked Miss Smart to check on our subscribers in the town. You guessed this morning when we were chasing up that address that I was hoping it would be a phoney."

McGrath continued to look sceptical, but he invited Charles to continue.

"Mac, when you were at school did you ever work from the answer in an algebraical problem?"

"I didn't do algebra," was the damping reply.

"Too bad!" Charles retorted. "It trains you in clear and logical thinking. Well, this business is like looking up the answer in the back of the book and working to fit it."

"I've heard about people looking at the back of a detective story."

"All right—it's like a detective story then. I think—or rather I'm sure—I know who killed Athol. Now I'm making the clues fit. That private detective Harry Jeffrey employed told me he had another client checking on Athol. The case was being handled from here in Sydney, but there was never any personal contact with the client. All business was done by letter and the address to which the investigating reports were sent was to Morton, care of Fisherton post office. Fisherton, you may remember, is on the same highway as Cranbilka."

"Long way to go to collect his mail," remarked McGrath.

"But not too long for someone accustomed to travelling the road and desirous of receiving letters anonymously, or parcels of chocolates. See this list I got from that confectioners in Melbourne—again, Morton care of Fisherton."

"All right," said McGrath, after a pause. "Who is this person who uses the name of Morton?"

Charles opened the book of verse again, and sat back in his chair at ease. "We'll wait for Miss Smart to bring that list of subscribers. Relax for a moment and I'll read some poetry."

McGrath put his head on one side. "You seem pretty sure of yourself, boy."

"I am. Listen—here's that thing Frances Turner recited that I asked Miss Smart to find. I was curious as to where she got it—real high-brow gibberish."

McGrath listened patiently, his gaze thoughtful as he stared at Charles.

"I bet you don't know what it means either." He turned a page, read a few more lines, then dwindled off hopelessly. "I can also bet that Athol made mincemeat of this in his review," he remarked, looking at the title on the spine of the jacket. "'Poems of Pain and Peace' by Dorothea Brand. Yes, it sounds like a woman, heaven help her!"

McGrath recrossed his legs and fumbled for another cigarette. Charles rang through to the secretary on the house-phone to enquire about the call to Cranbilka, but it had not yet come through.

"Call the exchange and tell them it's urgent," requested Charles. "By the way, this book of poems by Dorothea Brand—I'd like to have a look at the review. Can you dig it up? It's where? Oh good—thanks!"

He put down the house phone and turned to the title page. "Here's something to while away your boredom, Mac! Athol's unconsidered but frank opinions of the poetess's worth. Miss Smart pastes the reviews in the book. It cuts down filing, says the admirable creature. Listen to this as a fair sample of Athol's venom.

'"Poems of Pain and Peace" form a collection of agonising triteness. Both theme and treatment are of puerile sub-standard and the maudlin emoting, characteristic of a tiresome adolescent' et cetera et cetera . . . He goes on for a bit more along that line, but here's the last paragraph: 'Miss Brand—I cannot refer to her as the poetess—is a young woman who writes these painful pieces—' note the play on words, Mac—'from an invalid chair. Both the lady and her publishers hope to win our intellectual sympathy by exploiting her incapacitated state. It would be far better for the world of letters if the paralysis which, we are told, instigated the desire to write this pretentious mush, would mercifully spread to cut off any further attempts to abuse and distort the already long-suffering name of poetry.' Nice chap, wasn't he? I bet the poor woman never wrote another line."

McGrath gave his watch another glance. "Very entertaining. Will you excuse me, boy, if I make a phone call?"

"Go right ahead!" Charles gestured to the phone on the desk.

McGrath gave a sort of sheepish cough. "Well, as a matter of fact, it's the wife I want to ring."

Charles grinned and got up. "I'll go and see how Miss Smart is getting on."

"No, don't disturb yourself. I'll make a call from the board outside."

Charles was left alone until presently Miss Smart entered, holding a typewritten slip. "Here's that list of our subscribers at Cranbilka, Mr Carmichael."

He seized it eagerly, running his eye down the names. His expression changed ludicrously. "You're sure Morton gave no other name? Have we any other distributing agent in the town?"

"No, he is the only one."

"Damn!" he muttered in disappointment. "Did Mr McGrath see the list?"

The secretary nodded. "He made no comment."

There was a long pause as Charles stared ahead, frowning in a mixture of perplexity and irritation.

"Is there anything I can do, Mr Carmichael?"

"Yes," he exploded angrily. "You can find me the person in Cranbilka who had reason to hate Athol Sefton."

Miss Smart's brows rose a fraction. "That should be easy," she declared, leaning over to pick up the book on the desk. "What about this person?"

"Who? What do you mean?"

She leafed through it, looking for a particular page. "There happens to be a poem here about Cranbilka. I thought you knew, otherwise I would have drawn your attention to it earlier. Here it is—'The Call of Cranbilka'. It reads as though Dorothea Brand lives there."

Charles snatched the book from her. "By Jove!" he exclaimed on an exhaled breath. "Miss Smart, I can't thank you enough! Get me Morton on the telephone again. I'll speak to him myself. And tell Mac to stop nattering to his wife and to come back here."

There was an odd expression on the secretary's face. She said carefully, "It wasn't his wife Mr McGrath was ringing, but the police."

"Well, never mind! Just get me Morton as quickly as you can while I give poetess Brand's opus the closer study it warrants."

He came across one further clue in the book which, after a moment's consideration, made his eyes gleam with excitement. The call to Cranbilka came through just as McGrath re-entered the room. Charles was far too caught up by his discoveries to observe the watchful gaze which never strayed from him and the tensed, ever-ready set of the detective's solid frame as he seemed to lounge in a chair.

"Mr Morton? My name is Carmichael—associate editor of *Culture and Critic*. I want some information—yes, I know we rang before. This is something different. I've just been glancing through a book of poems by Dorothea Brand and came across one alluding to your town. Is she by any chance a local identity?"

Charles glanced meaningfully across at McGrath as he spoke. He frowned as the answer came over the wire. "What do you mean 'was'? Has she—what was that? What? Oh!" his voice dropped. There was a pause, then the voice on the line began to speak in a hesitant manner. The expression on Charles's face changed slowly as he listened.

"How very tragic!" he said finally. "But thank you for telling me. No, I certainly promise not to let it go any further. Just one other matter—I was intrigued by the dedication of Miss Brand's book. Do you happen to know—? Yes? Would you mind repeating the name? Thank you!"

Never were the two words more heartfeltly spoken. With a deep sigh that ended in a grin of pure triumph, Charles replaced the receiver.

McGrath's gaze remained unwinking as he asked pleasantly, "Well, boy, what now?"

Charles picked up the open book and read softly, "'Poems of Peace and Pain and Peace' by Dorothea Brand, dedicated 'to Drew, my beloved'. Mac, I've got it at last!"

"Got what, boy?"

"The explanation to the answer."

"Well, that's fine. Tell me all about it."

"Drew! Dorothea Brand's beloved! Andrew Turner. *He* murdered Athol, because Athol was the cause of Dorothea Brand's committing suicide. She killed herself because of that brutal review. According to Morton they were planning to be married."

He leaped up from his chair suddenly and began to pace to and fro. "It all fits in so perfectly. No coincidence, no loose ends and every step reasonable and logical. The only thing I feel sore about is that it was a woman's intuition that put me on the right track. It was Shelagh's idea to remove the probable suspects and what remained—the impossible—was the answer. And what could be more impossible than a honeymooning husband putting into the Duck and Dog seemingly on the off chance of getting a room. We know how he arranged for that room to be vacant. A phoney booking under the name of Morton then cancelled at the last minute."

"And was Mrs Turner a partner to this plot?" asked McGrath.

Charles paused. "No, I don't think so, but I think she has some suspicions. There were one or two things she said, and her manner was not that of a confident happy bride. Perhaps she was realising that her marriage was part of the scheme. She was her husband's alibi all the way—from arriving at Dunbavin to the actual killing of Athol. It is my belief he gave her a sleeping drug to cover leaving the bedroom to follow Athol and me. I know he had some tablets, because she gave me one when I couldn't sleep. But I think she might have recited that poem of Dorothea Brand's on purpose as a reproach to Turner. It wouldn't be very pleasant to know that you had been a tool to avenge another woman's death."

Suddenly he swung round to face McGrath and said urgently, "Mac, supposing Andrew knows that his wife has guessed! And now—now that she has served her purpose, he might be planning—Mac, you'd better have him picked up pretty smartly. They left Dunbavin, you know. There could be a car accident—perhaps a shooting accident. Come on, Mac! It's your job now. I've named the killer for you. It's up to you to see he doesn't kill again."

But McGrath did not move. "Now, don't get fussed, boy! Just take your time and tell me more of your notions."

There was a pause as Charles stared down at him incredulously. "Notions! You mean you don't—" he stopped, suddenly aware of the fact that McGrath did not believe in his theories and had no intention of being convinced by them.

He still thinks I'm the killer. He lied to me about ringing his wife, and now he's encouraging me to talk—playing for time until—

Charles pulled himself together. He knew that he was right—that Andrew Turner was the murderer. A desperate cunning took hold of him as he tried to plan a way of escape. He paced about the room again, pretending the excited triumph he had manifested before he realised what McGrath was thinking.

"Notions? You want to hear how I fitted the clues in?" he gabbled on heedlessly, while McGrath never moved his watchful gaze. He spoke about Turner and his probable route after leaving Dunbavin. When he darted into the store-room to consult the map, McGrath followed, his eyes going swiftly over the room to check any possible way of escape. There was a pair of windows but they were very small and set high in the wall and overlooking a sheer drop to a lane below.

Charles gave a quick casual glance at the door where McGrath stood. There was a key on the office side. He picked up a piece of doweling to use as a pointer. "I think Turner will travel in this direction, Mac. He is fairly confident that his tracks are covered; therefore it is all the more important to move in the usual direction instead of arousing suspicion by making straight for the bush. What do you think?"

"I'd say you were probably right," agreed the detective.

Charles moved the tip of the pointer. He noticed that his fingers were shaking slightly. "In that case, his way would follow the Diallong Highway from Dunbavin. Now, where the heck's Dunbavin?" He pretended to search for it. After a short hesitation, McGrath came alongside to indicate the position of the town but still staying between Charles and the door.

"Thanks, Mac. Now where do we go from there? Along this way? Yes, that's probably right. Turner would head towards Cranbilka once the job had been done. But what about this road cutting in? It goes in a straight line, practically to the border. According to my reasoning—if I were in Turner's shoes, I'd—" The pointer dropped from his hand and rolled along the floor.

Automatically, McGrath stooped to pick it up. At the same instant Charles gave him a violent push which sent the detective sprawling. In another instant he was out of the door, shutting and locking it.

"I won't say I'm sorry about this, Mac," he called rather breathlessly. "Since you don't believe me in theory, I'll have to bring the killer to you personally."

A muffled voice said, "You damned young fool—!" But Charles did not stop. He sped through Athol's office, locking the door after him, and out into the reception hall. At Miss Smart's door he paused and put his head in to say, "We're pushing off now, Miss Smart."

"Very well, Mr Carmichael. When will you be coming back?"

"In a day or so. Look after things as usual until you hear from me. Oh—and by the way—if anyone enquires for Mr McGrath, tell them he'll also be seeing them shortly." Charles turned his head. "That's about the message, isn't it, Mac?" he asked the empty hall.

Miss Smart made a note on a pad. "I'll do that."

"Thank you." Charles closed the door carefully, took a deep bracing breath and fled.

VII

Luck was with him the whole way. There was a taxi just getting rid of its fare outside the building, and the driver was actually agreeable to make the long trip to the aerodrome. At the airport, there was a vacancy on a plane just about to leave for Melbourne.

Trying to settle down to the irksome two-hour flight, Charles set himself the task of calculating how much time he would have. Unless McGrath was extraordinarily lucky—and Charles believed that he had the exclusive right to luck at the moment—he would not escape for some time. Miss Smart believed that he had left the building and would not hear him from the small closed room the other side of Athol's sound-proof office. Even if some of McGrath's detectives arrived, the message he had left would lead them to think that McGrath, for reasons best known to himself, was once again postponing the arrest.

It was dusk once more when the plane circled over Melbourne airport and dropped gently to the tarmac. Feeling tired and grimy, Charles was driven to his flat where he stayed only to shower and change his clothes. Then he took his car out and set it on the route back to Dunbavin. The petrol tank indicator was low, but he drove through the night until the needle barely flickered. Then he drew up on the side of the desolate country road and, dead tired, fell asleep behind the wheel.

The sun was up when he awoke, stiff and chilled. He got out and stamped up and down, swinging his arms and surveying a township which lay in the hollow a mile or so further on. He went back to the car and started to roll it. As it gathered momentum, he jumped in and coasted down the road, coming to a full stop a few yards from the first cottage of the township. There he left the car and went to look for a gasoline station and somewhere to eat.

An hour later he was on his way, a map spread out on the seat alongside. The route he planned was the one he had mapped out for McGrath, for it still seemed reasonable to him that Andrew Turner would go that way.

The Turners had left Dunbavin late Wednesday afternoon. They probably would not have travelled far before camping for the night. But on the following day—the day Charles and McGrath had spent chasing all over Sydney—they might have covered a considerable distance. With this thought in mind, Charles by-passed Dunbavin and pressed hard on the accelerator.

About eighty miles further on, he slowed down as another small township came into view, with a camping park attached to its sports oval. Here, with fingers crossed for the luck he believed would not desert him, he made some enquiries. To his immense satisfaction he learned that a young couple in a Holden utility truck had spent the night before last at the camping ground.

A grin of pure conceit crossed his face as the local storekeeper—who was also a caretaker for the park—volunteered further information that they intended making for a town two hundred miles on, in the environs of which they planned to stay. This particular town, Weerundi, was situated on a river which he himself had recommended as excellent for rainbow trout fishing. If Charles wished to meet up with them, he would most likely find them camped on a certain angle of the river three miles out of town—a spot which the storekeeper had gone to elaborate plans to identify as the young pair seemed so interested.

Charles thanked his informant fervently and got back into his car. The storekeeper ambled after him and leaned on the door. "In case they changed their minds, I suggest you make enquiries at Warner's store. I told them to look up old Bert if they wanted a licence or any tackle."

Charles thanked him again and thought what a wonderful place the country was. Any stranger in the district stood out like men from Mars, and their movements were automatically under surveillance. So intent was he on catching up with his quarry that it did not occur to him that he was a figure of interest and speculation too.

It was after midday when he left the camping ground. Back on the main road, he set the speedo climbing, making as good progress as the rugged surface of the secondary highway allowed. Towards evening he arrived at Weerundi, and drove slowly down the main street looking for Warner's store.

He was fortunate in finding it still open, the proprietor having been detained by a haggling buyer after fishing rods.

"Excuse me," said Charles, not disposed to being delayed at this juncture of the chase. "I'm in rather a hurry."

The buyer, a big man in grey flannels and a polo neck pullover, looked him over, then said grudgingly, "See what he wants then, Bert, I'll wait."

"Thanks," Charles acknowledged briefly and then addressed Bert. "The camp caretaker at Boyes told me to look you up. I'm looking for some—ah—friends of mine by the name of Turner—a young married couple. He said they would probably call here to obtain a fishing licence. Have you seen them?"

Bert pondered the question, rubbing his nose. "A young pair? Big, set-up fellow and a little, sort of softly spoken woman? Driving a Holden ute? Can't say as how their name was Turner though."

"It sounds like them. Your friend mentioned a spot on the river where he advised them to try their luck. Which road do I take?"

Bert massaged his chin. "I guess old Joe meant Angler's Point. You take the track behind the R. C. Church—rather a rough sort of road. It follows the river. If they're still there, you can't miss them."

"Thanks a lot," said Charles as he turned away. Then he thought of something else. "By the way, where is the police station in this town?"

There was a pause as Bert glanced over at the other customer, who had suddenly stopped making imaginary casts with the willow rod. "Police station? You want to know where the police station is? Why, that's just around the corner from here. But I reckon you won't find the sergeant in just now."

"I don't want to see him right away. Probably later—in fact, quite definitely later," Charles corrected himself, and then left the shop.

Dusk was now falling—a slow-encroaching film that is the beginning of the night-time in the country. Charles swerved and bumped over the narrow dirt track which led out to Angler's Point. Presently he saw a Holden utility backed in among the trees on the bank of the stream the track had been following. He drew up on the side of the track, switched off the engine and climbed out.

It was a still, quiet, warm evening. He could hear the splash and trickle of the water, and the hum of late summer insects. Advancing quietly towards the utility, he looked in the cabin. An ignition key dangled from the dash-board, its label bearing Turner's name and address. He felt a stab of anger when he saw the name Cranbilka, and remembered how hard he had worked to get hold of that name.

The scrub was thick, but he pushed his way through it as quietly as he could to where the ruddy glow of a fire was just visible. He could see a figure squatting beside it, and presently recognised Frances Turner. She was wearing faded jeans and a tartan shirt, and was busy scraping and filleting a fish. The fire shone on her intent little face. Charles thought she looked extraordinarily small and vulnerable. He glanced around carefully, but of Andrew there was no sign.

Suddenly Frances looked up. "Who's there?" she asked, her hands straining to the gun propped against a nearby tree.

Charles stepped out. "Don't be frightened," he said quietly.

She gave a gasp when she recognised him, followed by a hasty glance over her shoulder. "What are you doing here?"

"Where is your husband?"

"Andy? He is down at the river—fishing. What do you want with him?"

Charles came nearer. "I think you can guess," he said gently.

She looked up at him in silence for a moment. "I don't know

what you mean. Why have you followed us like this? Is there—is there anyone else with you?"

"No, I'm alone. If you are thinking of McGrath, I left him locked up in an office in Sydney."

"Locked up—! Are you joking at me? What were you doing in Sydney?"

"Discovering the identity of my uncle's murderer."

She jumped up and moved out of the firelight. "That is nothing to do with—with Andy," she said in her breathless, husky voice. "I can't think how—"

"Yes, you can! You've suspected all along that Andy killed Athol, haven't you?"

She bent her head and did not reply.

"Before he married you, Andy was in love with another girl in Cranbilka. Her name was Dorothea Brand and she wrote poetry. She had a volume published which Athol panned with more than his usual unpleasantness, making some wounding personal remarks which led her into taking her own life. After pursuing a cat-and-mouse torment, Andy finally ran Athol to earth at Dunbavin and killed him."

A long, shuddering sigh broke from the girl and she suddenly covered her face with her hands. Charles crossed to her quickly and put his hands on her shoulders. "Don't be distressed," he said quietly. "Be brave and face the facts—shocking though they are."

He continued to hold her while she trembled and cried noiselessly against him. She felt little and light and helpless. He put his arms around her slim body to support her more firmly, and she clung to him like child.

"Frances!" he spoke her name without meaning to, and she gave a child-like gulp of surprise and raised her head.

For a moment she stood in his arms silently, and she whispered hopelessly, "What am I going to do?"

"You must get away from your—from Andrew as quickly as you can. You're not safe if he knows you suspect him. I don't want to sound brutal, you poor little thing, but it is obvious he only married you for an alibi."

"You mean he would—he might—?" Charles nodded grimly and felt her shudder again.

"And you—what about you?" she asked, gripping the lapels of his coat with both hands. "What are you going to do?"

He hesitated for a moment. "I'm going to stay here to meet him."

"No, Charles, you mustn't! Let's slip away at once without seeing him."

He clasped her narrow wrists and gently put her away from him. "I'll be all right. I must stay. In some way or other, I've got to get him to admit his guilt. You see, the police think I killed Athol. This is my only chance."

"I won't leave you."

He felt in his pocket, drew out his car key and put it into her hand. "Take my car. It's down the track a bit. Go into the town and find the police station. It's round the corner from the store where you got your fishing licence. Tell the sergeant everything and bring him back here. If, by then, I haven't been able to—" he broke off and walked away from her to the other side of the clearing. Through the trees, he could see the faint glimmer of the stream and a shape moving along the steep, rock-strewn bank.

"Hey, Frankie!" came the faint call. Charles glanced over his shoulder. The girl had gone.

VIII

He went back to the fire, threw some twigs on it and waited. He could hear Andrew Turner clambering up the bank, and presently he appeared through the trees, dangling a pair of fair-sized trevally from one hand.

"Here's supper and breakfast, Frankie. Your old man has certainly got the game beaten."

"Good-evening, Turner!" Charles said from the shadows.

"Who's that?" asked the other quickly. "Oh, it's you, Carmichael. What on earth are you doing here? Hey, Frankie—guess who's blown in."

"Frances has gone," said Charles, advancing nearer the fire.

"Oh, you've seen her, have you? Where's she gone?"

"Into the town."

"She didn't say anything about going. What's she gone there for?"

"I told her to go. I want to have a talk with you—alone!"

"What about?" Turner asked defensively.

"Dorothea Brand," replied Charles quietly.

The other man seemed to stiffen. Then he began to dismantle his rod, concentrating on the task. "Has Frances been talking about Dorrie? She was her sister, you know."

"No, I didn't know. I first came across the name by reading a review Athol Sefton wrote of her book of poems. I made a few enquiries and learned about the—the subsequent tragedy."

"The old bastard!" exclaimed Turner violently. He appeared suddenly to realise what he had said and gave an uneasy laugh. "I suppose he had to write something. I can't understand why Dorrie took it so much to heart. She was a funny kid—frightfully highly-strung and sensitive. I suppose writing poetry—"

His voice dwindled away as Charles kept staring at him steadily. "I don't get what this is all about," he went on, more aggressively. "Why have you chased us all this way to talk about Dorrie? What have you been saying to my wife that she has gone off like this?"

"I told Frances to go because she is not safe staying with you."

"What do you mean—not safe?" the other shouted. "You've got a bloody nerve, you have. Don't you think I didn't see the way you were making up to Frances back at the Duck and Dog. What lies have you been spinning her?"

"No lies," replied Charles evenly. "Just facts of which she herself was suspicious."

"You've poisoned her mind against me in some way. Frankie knows I would never harm her."

"Maybe that's how you feel now, but supposing one day she made the mistake of letting you know her suspicions—what then? Supposing she became a danger to you?"

"I don't know what you mean."

"I think you do—only too well."

"You're crazy!" said Turner loudly. "Get the hell out of here or I'll—"

"Athol didn't know who you were," interrupted Charles, raising his voice. "You were quite safe, weren't you? It must have been strange that—knowing so much about Athol first and then meeting him face to face. What did you think of him that night, I wonder? Did the meeting soften or harden you in your resolve?"

"I hated his guts—just as I hate yours," said Turner furiously.

"Yes, I can well believe that. He was in top form that night. Is it any satisfaction to you to learn that Athol's behaviour then was mostly bravado? He was a worried, frightened man, Turner. You had succeeded wonderfully in your plans to torment him first. He had gone through a little hell already. Perhaps you might have been content if you had known. There were others who wanted to finish the job—Harry Jeffrey and Wilson and perhaps Adelaide Dougall."

"They all thought he was a stinker—I could see that."

"Yes, everyone hated Athol. I wasn't over-fond of him myself. But it had to be someone who hated Athol a bit more than average."

"What had to be?" demanded Turner fiercely. "Okay—go on with your nattering. You won't get any change out of me. I'd never met your bloody uncle before, and no one can make me say differently."

"Ah—that makes you feel so secure, doesn't it? But it won't work, Turner. You knew that Athol planned to duck-shoot and you persuaded Frances to take a sleeping dose, which, even if she awakened when you slipped from your room, would make her so heavy and confused as not to be sure of your departure. I've had one of those pills of yours and know their effect."

"It's a pity you didn't take the whole bottle," sneered Turner.

"You planned to take your own rifle when you followed Athol and me that morning," Charles went on. "A common enough type—a Wilding. But Ellis Bryce had a pair of them in his gunroom, which was quicker and, so you thought, safer to borrow than getting yours from your car or leaving it in your room for Frances to see. You took another precautionary measure by borrowing Athol's shoes. If the police did get suspicious and began looking for footprints you would be covered.

"You saw us put off in the boat and then selected a hidden position within range, from which you, as an expert shot, could not fail to be successful. There you waited until Athol stood up to fire at the ducks. It took you just one shot and what you had planned so carefully and cleverly was accomplished. You had murdered the man who had caused the death of Dorothea Brand."

Turner made a convulsive movement, then controlled himself. "Very clever, aren't you? You bump off your own uncle, hoping to make it look an accident and, when things start to get hot, you pin the blame on someone else. Well, you're not going to pin it on me, see? And I'm not going to open my mouth either. I'm going to find Frances and we are going home—back to Cranbilka, right away from swine like you and your uncle. And don't think to come after us, either. I'll fix it so that you won't be able to set foot in Cranbilka."

Charles watched him steadily. "You will never go back to Cranbilka with Frances," he said quietly. "It's almost the last scene, Turner. I sent Frances into the town to get the police. She should be back any minute, and then—" he turned aside, giving a fatalistic shrug.

A noise like that of an enraged animal came from Andrew Turner. He leapt at Charles, dragging him to the ground. They rolled over once or twice, locked together. There followed moments of confusion and struggle as each man strode to gain the offensive. The night was broken only by the sounds of their panting and grappling. Then Turner was astride of Charles, with his hand at his throat in a blind murderous rage.

Charles made desperate efforts to throw him off as he tugged at the other's fingers. He could feel the pressure on his wind-pipe growing firmer and there was a drumming in his head as though it would burst. When the explosions sounded, he thought it was part of his own death agony.

He came slowly back to reality after Turner's fingers had slipped from his throat. He lifted his head and watched with fascinated gaze as the big figure, which had been above him, turned in a slow heavy roll and settled into a quiet sprawling heap alongside him.

"Andy! Andy! Oh, what have I done!" cried Frances Turner, throwing herself beside the dead man. She burst into a flood of weeping, rocking herself to and fro.

With an effort, Charles tried to collect his thoughts. He leaned over and felt for Turner's heartbeat. His hand encountered a wet stickiness. "He's dead! How—?"

"I shot him! I shot him!" sobbed the girl. "I thought he was killing you, oh, Andy, Andy!"

Charles struggled to his feet and went to her. He drew her up, away from her dead husband and buried her head in his shoulder. He held her there quietly and firmly until the hysterical weeping ceased and she rested, spent from emotion, against him.

Suddenly, in her normal husky voice, she said hesitantly, "I was here all the time. I knew something like this might happen. I was so afraid—Andy—"

"Don't try to talk," said Charles soothingly, as her voice broke again and she began to tremble.

A sudden blinding light was focused on them, causing the girl to cry out in alarm. Then a well-known voice spoke out of the darkness beyond. "Well, boy! It seems as though I'm right on my cue."

IX

Back at Dunbavin's Duck and Dog, there had been much speculation as to the precipitate disappearance of Charles and McGrath. Shelagh Bryce, the only one with some idea of their whereabouts and the reasons thereto, maintained an attitude of unruffled and infuriating reticence and refused to be drawn into the discussion. But she went about her tasks in the hotel with a faint frown of worry on her smooth forehead and showed a tendency to jump when the telephone rang. Her father marked the slight disturbances of her habitual calm and showed an ironic concern.

Ellis was being more than ever tiresome, which was his way to work off irritation. He was completely in the dark as to the meaning of Charles's disappearance and found it galling. However, he was afforded some measure of reinstatement by being the one who answered Charles's telephone call on the night of the third day—the first news they had had since the meeting of the Dunbavin Reading Circle at the Spensers'. Charles explained briefly where he was, what had taken place and his intention to bring Frances Turner back to the hotel. McGrath would also return, as he felt Ellis and his household were entitled to a full explanation of the case.

"Well, well!" said Ellis, as he put back the receiver and turned to find Shelagh standing tensely at his elbow. "That was Charles, my dear—ringing from Weerundi. He's been having quite an interesting time up there. It seems he has caught up with poor Athol's killer at last—none other than our late guest, Andrew Turner."

"Andrew Turner! Did Charles say Mr McGrath had arrested him?"

"Charles was being very succinct. But I gathered from the brevity of his remarks that all is not well. Turner eluded arrest in that time-honoured way murderers have and he is most concerned about the little widow. He wants you to care for her for a few days. They will be here this evening, so go and break the news to Grace while I tell the rest of the ghouls."

Ellis then retired to the bar, where he spent a most enjoyable day pretending that it was Andrew Turner whom he had had in mind when he had declared earlier that he could guess who had shot Athol Sefton. There was relief on several faces at the news and the guests unbent towards each other as suspicions evaporated. Speculation now turned on how Charles and McGrath had tracked Turner down, and it was an eager, avid audience that awaited the appearance of the three principals.

Their entrance, if they had felt inclined to mind such matters, could not have been better timed. They came in when the whole household was drinking after-dinner coffee in the lounge. The exclamations of welcome were topped by Margot Stainsbury's inimitable little shriek which she gave at the sight of Charles's bruised face.

"Never mind about that now," he said shortly, guiding Frances solicitously to a chair. He bent over her, whispering, and looked up with a wistful smile. Then he straightened and asked, "Where is Shelagh?"

"Here," replied a quiet even voice. The others had gathered around McGrath at the far end of the room. Charles went to her with one hand outstretched. "Well, the woman's instinct was right," he admitted, smiling. "I don't know how to thank you for the tip."

"I'm glad you found some use for it," she returned coolly, looking beyond him at the small huddled figure he had left. "What is to happen now?"

His smile changed to a frown of concern. "I think Frances should go to bed, don't you? Perhaps we should get old Spenser to see her."

From across the room, the girl caught what he was saying. "No, please, I feel perfectly all right. And I'd much rather stay here than go to bed." The group near McGrath stopped talking and turned at the sound of the gentle husky voice. Frances glanced at them fleetingly. "But please don't let me stop you from—from any discussion you may wish to have. I'd much rather stay here and listen, than go to my room and wonder what you were saying."

Mrs Dougall beamed approvingly. "You're perfectly entitled to stay—and a brave gal to face up to things!" The Major made strangulated noises of endorsement through his moustache, and Adelaide, ready tears of sympathy shining in her eyes, crossed the room to sit beside Frances.

"As far as I'm concerned," announced the American, his jaw pugnacious as he gazed at McGrath, "your husband did everyone a good turn, and you mourn our hero, not a villain."

"I ag—ag—" stammered Wilson earnestly.

"Mr Wilson agrees with Mr Jeffrey's sentiments," supplied Ellis in bored tones.

"Well, I don't!" announced Jerry trenchantly. "Oh, I admit Athol was a swine and all that, but you can't go bumping people off because you've got a hate against them. Furthermore, you can't make a hero out of a man who was unable to face the music. Suiciding when you're caught is a poor show, I think!"

"Jerry!" said Charles furiously.

McGrath stepped into the centre of the room. "All right, boy! Don't get hot and bothered. You're sure you're all right, Mrs Turner?"

Her voice shook a little as she answered, "Yes, please go on. They'll have to know it sooner or later."

The detective addressed Jerry. "I don't know whether it will put Turner back on his pedestal for you, but the truth is he didn't suicide. He was shot—by Mrs Turner."

"We were fighting," Charles enlarged hastily. "Frances only intended to wound him, but—" He broke off as a quiet sob came from the girl. Abruptly she buried her head in Adelaide's receptive shoulder.

"You mean she saved your life?" asked Margot, her eyes open wide. "You must be terribly, terribly grateful to her, Chas."

"I am," he said quietly, and a respectful silence fell.

"Well, now!" said McGrath genially. "Having got over the final hurdle, perhaps we might as well go back to the beginning."

"Yes, go on," said Frances, raising her head. "Now you all know why I wanted to be here. I couldn't bear the thought of your talking about what I had done behind my back."

"The point that troubles me," remarked Ellis, as though pondering a great question, "is if Andrew is a hero, can Frances be a heroine when she killed him?"

"Have some coffee, Father," suggested Shelagh, who had taken a cup to Frances.

"My daughter is rebuking me for ill-timed facetiousness. Do continue, Mr McGrath! We are all agog as to how you tracked down poor Athol's killer."

"Charles is better qualified to give you that explanation," said McGrath handsomely.

"You may have the privilege," Charles conceded with a grin. "The only thing I do want to know is how you got out of the storeroom in Athol's office. I locked Mac in because he didn't seem to believe me about Turner and I wanted a free hand," he explained to the others.

Without rancour, McGrath related the details of his escape. He had managed, after much patient manipulation of various extempore lock-picking tools, to eject the store-room key to the ground and draw it under the door. Once in Athol's office, he had tried the telephone, but Miss Smart had switched the exchange line to the board before leaving the office. The only move was to attract the attention of someone below in the street. He attracted so much attention that the flying squad, a fire brigade cart and a minister of religion arrived on the scene, all equally convinced that he was a would-be suicider. It took quite some time to explain his position, but at the first available opportunity he set into motion a new plan of investigation to check on Charles's own enquiries. He then set off in hot pursuit and was, in fact, only a short distance behind him, having travelled through the night Charles spent at the roadside.

The camp attendant at Boyes proved as helpful to McGrath as he had been to Charles, and it was from his store that the detective had rung through to the police at Weerundi asking him to keep a look-out for a young chap enquiring about the Holden utility. The Weerundi sergeant stationed himself as an interested buyer at Warner's store, listened to Charles's story, and then waited for McGrath so as to conduct him to the camp at Angler's Point.

Charles again interposed hastily at this juncture, and told his listeners of the various moves he had taken after fleeing from the Spensers' party.

"It was as I said at the beginning," remarked Ellis, with complacent sapience. "Athol was murdered because of a disgruntled writer to whom he had given a poor review."

Charles allowed him his pleasure. "Yes, I remember you said something of that kind."

"At one stage I seem to recall your saying any one of us could be guilty," said Jeffrey, with a grin.

"Did you, Ellis?" queried Margot, with a shriek of protest. "Even I—you horrid man?"

"Even you, my dear."

While they were bickering amiably, Charles went back to Frances. "Are you sure you are all right? They don't mean to be brutal, but I don't see how you can bear it."

"I'm perfectly all right," she repeated, smiling gratefully at his concern. "And Miss Dougall is being so kind." Adelaide grew red with the pleasure of being acknowledged.

McGrath's voice broke through a clearing in the conversation. "There now seems only one problem that has been left unanswered."

Charles turned round quickly. "What is that?"

"The one and only problem as far as I'm concerned. The reason why I was sent down here in the first place. Who murdered Mrs Paula Sefton?"

X

A sudden quietness fell over the room—a silence which seemed to manifest uneasiness and regret at having lowered guards too soon.

"Oh, Mac!" said Charles disgustedly. "You're not going to start that all over again, are you? Does it rankle because I showed you the way to Athol's killer?"

"Not in the least, boy," the other returned amiably. "I am exceedingly grateful to you for putting me on the right track. But I very much doubt if Turner murdered Sefton."

"You doubt it!" repeated Charles incredulously. "Have you gone mad?"

A buzz of talk broke out which Shelagh silenced with a crisp, "Be quiet, and let Mr McGrath explain."

The detective looked at her quizzically. "Thank you, Miss Bryce. I had a high regard for your intelligence right from the start. It's a pity Charles does not appreciate it." Then he addressed the others apologetically. "I'm sorry to upset your sense of false security, but I was never very interested in Sefton's death. My job here primarily is to enquire into the death of his wife, which took place some months ago. One always starts with a husband in such a case—hence my arrival in Dunbavin."

"The natural starting point," observed Ellis languidly.

"Yes, Sefton seemed the obvious culprit in an obvious case— the rich cantankerous invalid wife and the bon-vivant husband of limited means. Unfortunately I arrived too late to ask him if he had done the obvious in poisoning his wife. There was, however, a substitute suspect with whom I was able to get on intimate terms almost at once.

"Through Charles I arrived at the Duck and Dog, where I learned that his story of your divers dislikes of Sefton was not unfounded. He had also told me that his uncle's behaviour just prior to his apparent accidental death was that of a man suffering some sort of fear—though not necessarily of his life. There had been vague threatening messages and so on. When the possibility occurred to me that it was Charles whom Athol suspected of sending the messages, my case against him strengthened."

"You've got everything utterly upside down," Charles said loudly.

"It would seem so," McGrath admitted. "But it was you he was worried about. You see, Charles, Mrs Sefton was murdered for no other reason than that Athol Sefton would be accused of her death. He dared not lodge a complaint about the messages to the police. Your uncle suspected that she had been poisoned and the only way that could have happened was through the chocolates which you periodically sent your aunt. For a while he must have considered the possibility of your aunt's arranging her own death and the subsequent messages—hence his talk of ghosts to Miss Stainsbury."

"Turner knew I sent chocolates to Aunt Paula. Lots of people probably knew, for that matter. His initial plan of revenge was to have Athol suffer for a crime he did not commit. When that failed he decided to come after him personally."

"So that was why Athol had his wife cremated," remarked Ellis, "I presume he was able to fix the death certificate because of her well-known chronic bad health. How frustrating for you, Charles!"

Charles made a gesture of weary resignation. "How do you talk like that, Father!" exclaimed Shelagh. "Athol came to a wrong conclusion, Charles. It wasn't you he should have been afraid of, but—" She broke off as she realised where her burst of indignation was leading her.

"Go on!" invited McGrath. "I feel sure you know."

The girl looked across at him tensely. "Perhaps I do know, but supposing I am wrong? After all, it could only be a guess."

"Go ahead and guess then. You put Charles on the right track, but he took a wrong turning."

"All right!" said Shelagh, throwing up her hand. "It wasn't you Athol feared, Charles, not someone he knew."

"It was Turner," he said impatiently. "Even supposing Aunt Paula was murdered, he still fits."

"No, he doesn't," she contradicted gently. "There is one item Andrew Turner never fitted—Athol's shoes!"

There was a puzzled silence which McGrath broke by saying, "Go right ahead, Miss Bryce. You need have no fear of making a mistake."

"She is her father's daughter," observed Ellis irrepressibly. "Shelagh, my dear, tell us quickly. Who did fit Athol's shoes, by whatever bearing they may have on this most drawn-out affair?"

"The person who killed Athol wore his shoes to disguise footprints," explained Charles slowly, and there was a look of dawning uneasiness in his eyes.

"Then it couldn't have been Turner," said the American. "He was a much bigger man than your uncle."

"Don't tell me it is going to lapse into a Cinderella farce where we all have to try on Athol's shoes," implored Ellis. "Mr McGrath— since my daughter seems so reluctant to speak, won't you, please?"

"I'm only reluctant," said Shelagh quietly, "because it is not my place to be pointing the accusing finger. Charles, you must know now. Remember those shoes of Athol's—they were laced! Who could have removed them after use without undoing the laces?"

"Only someone with a much smaller foot than Athol."

"A woman, Charles!"

He gazed around the room wildly. "Don't look at me like that, young man!" boomed Mrs Dougall, sitting up straight. Nearby, Margot gave a little cry and put up her hands as though protecting herself.

Charles turned back to McGrath. "But Turner practically admitted everything!"

"Everything? Did he actually say he killed Athol?"

"No, no, he didn't, but—Mac, I must be right!"

"You took the wrong turning, boy," said McGrath gently. He walked across the room to where Adelaide and Frances Turner sat.

"I have a warrant for your arrest for the murders of Mrs Paula Sefton and her husband, Athol. I must warn you—"

"Adelaide!" cried Mrs Dougall.

"No, not Adelaide," snapped Shelagh over the sudden roar. "Frances Turner!"

With the stunned gaze of the room upon her, Frances sat up straight in her chair, staring at McGrath with wide grave eyes. "I don't understand what you mean. Andy—"

"Mrs Turner!" interrupted McGrath wearily, "you are a consummate actress, particularly in the role of the injured, helpless innocent. But I am a middle-aged policeman who has come up against your type before. You fooled your husband and you fooled Charles, but you can't fool me."

She began to weep softly. "After all I have been through—"

"Keep your tears for the jury," he recommended, putting a hand under her elbow and raising her up. "It will be for them to decide who had the stronger motive for revenging Dorothea Brand's suicide—her devoted sister or the man that sister knew probably never had any intention of marrying a paralytic. Proof of the one-sidedness of that affair can be seen in the way you were able to get Andrew to marry you. It is my belief that you did that not only as a cover but also so that if anything went wrong—as it did—Andrew would get his just deserts for not returning your sister's devotion."

The tears slipped down her cheeks unchecked. "You're making a terrible mistake. I loved Andy, but I know now that he was only using me. I've never been out of Cranbilka before—before my honeymoon. But Andy used to go everywhere on account of his contracting business. He often went through Fisherton."

"Why do you mention Fisherton, Mrs Turner?"

Her big eyes, wet with tears, flickered. "That's where—didn't Charles say that—"

"Charles did not say the name, Mrs Turner. In his account he merely said that to preserve anonymity, the murderer gave a false name and a post office address some distance from Cranbilka.

Your late husband was easily deceived by some pretext into collecting your mail—which included not only reports from the private enquiry agency you employed to check on the Seftons, but also supplies of chocolates from the Melbourne confectioner that Charles patronised for his aunt. The report I received on you from Cranbilka says that prior to your marriage you were employed as an assistant to the local chemist. We have asked him to check on any dangerous pharmaceutical ingredients that might be missing."

Frances turned her head. "Charles!" she called imploringly. Charles was sitting slumped in a chair looking lost and dejected. Shelagh bent over him. "You mustn't even look at her," she advised quietly.

McGrath surveyed him kindly from across the room. "When you get into the crime game professionally, boy, you learn never to let your emotions become involved. I grew to like you, Charles, but I still would not have hesitated to arrest you. What you told me in Sydney was going to be your last chance. Luckily for you, your theories stood up to investigation and turned out to be right in every detail except the exact identity of the killer. I am full of admiration for what you did, boy!"

Charles raised his eyes. "Thanks, Mac—but are you quite—sure?"

"Quite sure, boy. You need have no remorse. Mrs Turner has her head screwed on properly—you can tell by the way she is keeping up her act. The prosecution is in for a tough time. She may even get off at her trial. Heaven help you if she still affects you in the same way then, for remember this—she had no hesitation in planting that Wilding on you and she made a scapegoat out of her husband even to the extent of killing him! In the meantime—here, Miss Bryce, you look after the foolish fellow!"

"I'll do that," Shelagh promised, a deep, warm note in her voice. "Charles, look at me!"

Ellis's eyes goggled and Miss Bryce, coming in to collect the coffee cups, fell into mild hysterics as Shelagh took Charles's face in her hands and kissed him long and efficiently.

"Why, Shelagh!" exclaimed Charles idiotically, when he was able to speak. He did not notice that McGrath had led Frances Turner from the room.

THE END

MORE FROM JUNE WRIGHT

MURDER IN THE TELEPHONE EXCHANGE

"A classic English-style mystery . . . packed with detail and menace."—*Kirkus Reviews*

June Wright made quite a splash in 1948 with her debut novel. It was the best-selling mystery in Australia that year, sales outstripping even those of the reigning queen of crime, Agatha Christie.

When an unpopular colleague at Melbourne Central is murdered – her head bashed in with a buttinsky, a piece of equipment used to listen in on phone calls – feisty young "hello girl" Maggie Byrnes resolves to turn sleuth. Some of her co-workers are acting strangely, and Maggie is convinced she has a better chance of figuring out the killer's identity than the stodgy police team assigned to the case, who seem to think she herself might have had something to do with it. But then one of her friends is murdered too, and it looks like Maggie is next in line.

Narrated with verve and wit, this is a mystery in the tradition of Dorothy L. Sayers, by turns entertaining and suspenseful, and building to a gripping climax. It also offers an evocative account of Melbourne in the early postwar years, as young women like Maggie flocked to the big city, leaving behind small-town family life for jobs, boarding houses and independence.

(336 pages, with a new introduction by Derham Groves)

SO BAD A DEATH

When *Murder in the Telephone Exchange* was reissued in 2014, June Wright was hailed by the *Sydney Morning Herald* as "our very own Agatha Christie," and a new generation of readers fell in love with her inimitable blend of intrigue, wit, and psychological suspense – not to mention her winning sleuth, Maggie Byrnes.

Maggie makes a memorable return to the fray in *So Bad a Death*. She's married now, and living in a quiet Melbourne suburb. Yet violent death dogs her footsteps even in apparently tranquil Middleburn. It's no great surprise when a widely disliked local bigwig (who also happens to be her landlord) is shot dead, but Maggie suspects someone is also targeting the infant who is his heir. Her compulsion to investigate puts everyone she loves in danger.

(288 pages, with a new introduction by Lucy Sussex, plus her fascinating interview with June Wright from 1996)

ALSO FROM DARK PASSAGE BOOKS

PETER DOYLE

Peter Doyle's crime novels, featuring irresistible antihero Billy Glasheen, brilliantly explore the criminal underworld, political corruption, and the explosion of sex, drugs, and rock'n'roll in postwar Australian life, and have earned him three Ned Kelly Awards, including a Lifetime Achievement Award in 2010. Two titles are currently available from Dark Passage, with a new novel, *The Big Whatever*, scheduled for 2015.

THE DEVIL'S JUMP

August 1945: the Japanese have surrendered and there's dancing in the streets of Sydney. But Billy Glasheen has little time to celebrate; his black marketeer boss has disappeared, leaving Billy high and dry. Soon he's on the run from the criminals and the cops, not to mention a shady private army. They all think he has the thing they want, and they'll kill to get hold of it. Unfortunately for Billy, he doesn't know what it is . . . but he'd better find it fast.

> "Peter Doyle does for Sydney what Carl Hiaasen does for Miami."
> —Shane Maloney

GET RICH QUICK

Sydney in the 1950s. Billy Glasheen is trying to make a living, any way he can. Luckily, he's a likeable guy, with a gift for masterminding elaborate scenarios—whether it's a gambling scam, transporting a fortune in stolen jewels, or keeping the wheels greased during the notorious 1957 tour by Little Richard and his rock 'n' roll entourage.

But trouble follows close behind—because Billy's schemes always seem to interfere with the plans of Sydney's big players, an unholy trinity of crooks, bent cops, and politicians on the make. Suddenly he's in the frame for murder, and on the run from the police, who'll happily send him down for it. Billy's no sleuth, but there's nowhere to turn for help. To prove it wasn't him, he'll have to find the real killer.

> "An absolute gem . . . a marvellous read and a truly distinctive piece of Australian crime writing."—*Sydney Morning Herald*

> "Think of a hopped-up James M. Cain."—*Kirkus Reviews*

ALSO FROM DARK PASSAGE BOOKS

G.S. MANSON – *Coorparoo Blues & The Irish Fandango*

Written in the spare, plain-spoken style of all great pulp fiction, G.S. Manson's series featuring 1940s Brisbane P.I. Jack Munro captures the high stakes and nervous energy of wartime, when everything becomes a matter of life and death.

BRISBANE, 1943. Overnight a provincial Australian city has become the main Allied staging post for the war in the Pacific. The tensions – social, sexual, and racial – created by the arrival of thousands of US troops are stirring up all kinds of mayhem, and Brisbane's once quiet streets are looking pretty mean.

Enter Jack Munro, a World War I veteran and ex-cop with a nose for trouble and a stubborn dedication to exposing the truth, however inconvenient it is for the -powers that be. He's not always a particularly good man, but he's the one you want on your side when things look bad.

When Jack is hired by a knockout blonde to find her no-good missing husband, he turns over a few rocks he's not supposed to. Soon the questions are piling up, and so are the bodies. But Jack forges on through the dockside bars, black-market warehouses, and segregated brothels of his roiling city, uncovering greed and corruption eating away at the foundations of the war effort.

Then Jack is hired to investigate a suspicious suicide, and there's a whole new cast of characters for him to deal with – a father surprisingly unmoved by his son's death, a dodgy priest, crooked cops, Spanish Civil War refugees – and a wall of silence between him and the truth, which has its roots deep in the past. Friends, enemies, the police – they're all warning Jack to back off. But he can't walk away from a case: he has to do the square thing.

"Great historical detail of wartime Australia mixed with the steady pace of sex and violence . . . keeps the pages turning."—*Brisbane Courier-Mail*

"Rough and gritty, but also vital."—*The Age*

DARK PASSAGE BOOKS
CHECKLIST

also available as ebooks

darkpassagebooks.com
facebook.com/versechoruspress